by

Catherine Winchester

What You Wish For

by

Catherine Winchester

This is a work of fiction. Names, characters, places, and incidents, other than those clearly in the public domain, are the product of the author's imagination or are used fictitiously, and any resemblance to actual persons, living or dead, business establishments, events, or locales is entirely coincidental.

Acknowledgements

To everyone who commented on this story and helped me believe that it was actually not too bad!

To Margot, for patiently editing books that she has no interest in and for never losing her patience when I make the same mistakes again and again (and again).

And finally to my readers, who make what I do so worthwhile.

Preface

Most authors write because we love it. Sure, some probably do it solely for a paycheck but most of us love our craft and would continue to write even if we never sold another book. Sometimes we write things that we don't believe will be saleable; as a writing exercise, to help us understand a character better or even just for fun. This book started out as the latter.

I just couldn't get the idea of living in historical romance out of my head; would it really be as romantic as TV and books make it out to be? Women had almost no rights back then, how would a modern woman who is used to the freedom's we have today, cope when those kinds of restraints were placed upon her?

The idea kept plaguing me and eventually I had no choice but to sit down and write the story. I didn't think it would ever be good enough to publish so I began to post it online and to my immense surprise, it proved surprisingly popular, even with people who are unfamiliar with the book my heroine finds herself trapped in, Elizabeth Gaskell's North and South

So (two rewrites and three edits later) the rest as they say, is history!

I hope you enjoy this story. It won't change your life or enrich your soul but I sincerely hope it will entertain you for a while.

Chapter One

Carrie Preston looked at her reflection in the mirror and sighed. She honestly didn't know why she was going to all this trouble, getting herself made up and doing her hair just so. Her Aunt Imelda was not two weeks dead, surely she deserved to look a little downtrodden. But of course, that wasn't the Preston way.

No matter what was happening in your life, whether your husband had just left you, your business had collapsed or your child was ill, the show must go on. Heaven forbid any Preston appear in public showing visible signs of distress!

Carrie hated her family and yet, for an easy life when she was around them, all too often she played along.

Aunt Imelda hadn't been like that; she was the black sheep of the family, the renegade who was whispered about behind closed doors. She had been a free spirit, free with her men (scandalous!) free with her money (hence always poor) but most importantly to Carrie, she had also been free with her love and affection, something Carrie got precious little of from her parents.

She hadn't been allowed to see Imelda until she was seven years old when for some unknown reason, her mother finally took the children to see their aunt. Carrie never did understand why they were suddenly introduced to this relative who they had never heard of before but she was ever so glad of it.

Today was the reading of her will and Carrie had been told she had to be there, meaning that she was mentioned in the will. She knew her aunt had no money so she wasn't expecting to leave the solicitors office with new found wealth but she was hoping that Imelda had left her something of sentimental importance, like her handwritten recipe books. God, how she had loved those things, scribbling new recipes on each page as she found them or made them up. Some contained ingredients that weren't exactly legal but Carrie wasn't planning on using them for reference, rather as something to remember her aunt by.

As she looked at herself in the mirror, she felt like a hypocrite, for though she claimed to despise her superficial family, here she was dressed in Christian Dior, wearing thousands of pounds of diamonds, with flawless make up and smelling like Chanel No5.

Imelda would have turned up with no makeup, in her long, flowing, handmade skirts, her wooden beaded jewellery and smelling of incense. Carrie could only wish for such bravery.

She looked up to the ceiling, where she imagined her aunt would be looking down upon her from.

"Sorry, Imm, maybe next time," she apologised.

Carrie didn't really believe in ghosts or souls or an afterlife. Of course she didn't exactly disbelieve either but what mattered here was that Imelda believed in all that kind of stuff and if she could be watching events on earth wherever she was, then she surely would be, and probably having a right good laugh at her prissy baby sisters family!

"Wish me luck," she told the ceiling as she slipped her makeup into her handbag, just in case she needed any touch ups while she was out. Her mother hadn't been pleased when she'd cried at the funeral and hadn't brought extra makeup with which to repair the damage.

Carrie had started talking to her aunt the day after she died, just trying to say goodbye really since she hadn't made it to the hospital in time, but it had comforted her to do so and ever since she had aimed the odd comment at her aunt, hoping that somehow Imelda would hear her.

Though he was not yet thirty, Daniel Winston was a very grave looking man. Carrie sat silently, almost afraid he would tell her off if she dared to laugh as he read the will. And laugh she truly wished she could.

"To my sister, Patricia Preston, I leave my collection of marijuana plants in the hope that you will learn to lighten up," Mr Winston read in his serious, queen's English accent.

Carrie bit her lip to keep from laughing.

"To my niece, Annabel, I leave my art work. I know you think they are rubbish but I thought that you might be able to laugh at them in my death as you did while I was alive, for joy is sadly lacking in your life."

Imelda went on to insult a few more people posthumously but to a few she left boxes wrapped in brown paper that were to be opened in private. Carrie received one such box, no larger than a shoe box really but, she hoped, chock full of happy memories.

She slid the box onto her lap where she held it protectively. She knew her mother and sister would be dying to know what was in there but opening it was something she wanted to do on her own.

Finally Mr Winston finished reading the will and with a very pointed, "Well," he made it quite clear that the outrageous comments had not been his idea.

"If you have any questions, please feel free to ask

me before you leave or make an appointment with my secretary," he said, standing, obviously pleased that his ordeal was over.

Carrie had arrived late and so, other than a few nods of welcome, she hadn't actually spoken to her family yet. She got up, hoping to get out of there before she was accosted but she wasn't to be that lucky a second time.

"Dozy old bat," Annabel said, linking her arm through her sister's. "Honestly, I knew coming here would be a waste of time."

"Then why did you come?" Carrie asked.

"Because I was asked to."

Carrie rolled her eyes, wondering if her sister had ever had an original thought.

"So, what do you think she left you? Her crystal ball? Her tarot cards?" she cackled like a witch.

"It's not heavy enough to be her crystal ball." Carrie answered simply.

"Oh come on, don't be so depressing! We all knew this was coming, it wasn't like the cancer came out of nowhere."

"No, but I wasn't expecting her to go downhill so fast."

"So what, you'd have cancelled your holiday if you had known?"

"Actually yes."

"I'll bet Mark would have loved that!" Annabel snorted.

"Mark would have understood," Carrie argued, though in all honesty she wasn't sure he would.

"When are you two going to get married, anyway?" her mother said, coming up behind them as they exited onto the street. "You've been together almost three years; it's time he made an honest woman of you."

"I've told you before, not until I finish Uni, at the earliest."

Her mother tutted, which Carrie translated to mean *'Why do you need a degree when you've got a rich stockbroker who is willing to marry you and keep you in the lifestyle to which you are accustomed?'*

"Mum, I've got to go," she said, withdrawing her arm from her sister and turning to face her mother. "I've got a paper due tomorrow and I'm so far behind it's unreal."

"I wish you wouldn't use such common language," Patricia scowled.

If 'unreal' upset her, Carrie wondered what hearing her banter after a few pints at the Student Union would do to her mother.

"Aren't you going to open it?" her sister pointed at the box.

"It's probably just rubbish like you said; I'll open it when I don't have a deadline."

Before they could argue, Carrie kissed their cheeks and dashed off across the road towards her car.

Patricia shook her head in consternation. "Honestly, that girl."

"She'll settle down soon," Annabel assured her mother. "She's just sowing a few wild oats in college; she'll be fine once she graduates."

"I hope so. Anyway, darling, how are the twins and that lovely husband of yours?"

"Oh, they're fine. We just got a new au pair actually."

As soon as Carrie got home she stripped off her suit, pulled on jeans and a jumper, put her hair up into a messy twist with a butterfly clip and poured herself a large glass of wine. She took a long sip and sighed, letting the stress of the day go.

She was home, safe at last and free to be herself. She settled down on the sofa, turned the CD player on and set about opening the box.

On top was a letter.

Darling Carrie, if you're reading this I have either eloped with George Clooney, never to be heard from again and have been declared dead after seven years.

Carrie smiled, for Imelda's crush on George Clooney was legendary.

Or, as I fear, I really am dead and you've just been forced to listen to that arse, Winston, read my will without a trace of the humour it deserves.

If it is the second option, I just want you to know how very much I love you, and how much you mean to me. If I could have had a child, I would have wanted you.

In this box is just some old junk really, things that are of importance only to you and me. There's my favourite pictures of us, some nic nacs that have precious memories and one more thing that is very dear to me.

The amethyst earrings you'll find in here were a gift from a great friend of mine when I was in my twenties. You'll have seen me wear them a lot, especially when you were young. Now, I know it sounds crazy but those earrings gave me my heart's desire. No, I won't tell you what that was, but let's just say my life would have been very different if it hadn't been for those earrings and I hope they will give you as much joy as they have brought me. And if you don't believe a word of this, then just treat them as my favourite pair of earrings and something I now pass down to you.

Wherever I am now, always know that I'm looking out for you, my darling girl.

All my love,

Aunt Immy.

Carrie sighed and wiped the tears from her eyes before she put the letter away and began going through the contents of the box. Imelda was right, it was mostly a bunch of junk, like the teeny teddy bear Carrie had wasted twenty pounds trying to win at a funfair. She'd wanted the giant teddy but alas her skills meant that she could only win this two inch tall one. Still, they'd had a great time trying.

She looked through the pictures, alternately smiling at the happy memories they brought to mind and crying, for they would be unable to make any more such memories.

Finally she reached the jewellery box and opened it to see the tear drop amethyst earrings that Imelda used to wear all the time.

She wondered what her aunt's heart's desire had been for a while, then she wondered what her own heart's desire would be. Not Mark, that was for sure.

Mark was okay, but he was too superficial to ever settle down with. Like her family, he valued money above all else, whereas Carrie wanted to become an artist or a teacher. Something meaningful where she could really help people. Mark didn't understand that desire. He wasn't evil or anything, and when they had first met and he'd still been in his final year of Uni, he'd actually been rather nice. It was only since leaving and getting a job at the brokerage that he seemed to have gained such a love of money.

She knew she should dump him but like the coward that she was, she couldn't face the grief she would surely get from her family over it, for they adored Mark. She had been planning to tell him when they got back from their holiday actually, but as soon as she turned her mobile phone on once they had landed she'd received the text message telling her that Imelda had passed away.

She would break it off with Mark soon; she just needed to regain some of her strength first.

She traced the earrings with her fingers, wondering who had given them to her aunt; then on impulse she took her diamond earnings off and slipped them into her purse for safekeeping, then put the amethyst ones on instead. They were infinitely cheaper than the diamond clusters that they had replaced and yet priceless by comparison.

Finally, depressed enough for one evening, she put the lid back on the box of memories and put it out of sight for a while. She picked up her dog-eared copy of North and South off the coffee table and settled down on the sofa to read a little more of it.

This book was like chocolate to her, her comfort food in literary form, a safe haven that she could dip into whenever she needed a respite from her troubles or just a distraction for a while.

Carrie awoke the next morning and realised she'd fallen asleep on the sofa. She rubbed her eyes and was starting to regret that third glass of wine. Still, as she had class this morning, she really should make a move to get up and at 'em.

She closed the book that was lying on her chest, swapped it for the TV remote on the coffee table and turned the TV onto News24 while she attempted to rouse herself into a mobile state of consciousness. The clock on the corner of the screen told her that she had about an hour to get to her first lecture; plenty of time.

Finally she summoned the necessary willpower to get up and she turned the kettle on while she brushed her teeth, took a lightening quick shower and changed into clean jeans and jumper. By the time she made it back to the kitchen the kettle was boiled and she made herself an industrial strength coffee and sat back down on the sofa while she sipped it, hoping that the caffeine might help her tap into an as yet undiscovered energy reserve.

It did help clear some of the cobwebs from her mind but the truth was, she was depressed; that's why she'd had the third glass of wine and that was why she constantly felt as if she had no energy these past two weeks.

It wasn't just her aunt dying, although that was probably the catalyst for how she felt. She just felt like she was stuck in a rut, living in an apartment bought by her family, studying for a degree she hadn't wanted and would probably never use. Dating a man she didn't particularly like any more and basically just living a life that she didn't want.

She was studying literature because that was deemed a suitable subject for a society wife. She liked literature, obviously, but it wasn't something she wanted to make a career of. She had wanted to study engineering but her family had vetoed that idea, refusing to support her through university if she did choose that subject. Of course she had caved. If she did manage to break away from her family when she left university, she didn't really want to start her new life saddled with massive student loans.

It was cowardly. She was cowardly. She wished that she had her aunt's strength but the truth was simply that she was weak and unable to stand up for what she wanted.

How much simpler things were in books where any of life's obstacles could be overcome. Well, except for the downbeat novels but Carrie preferred books with happy endings. How she would love to just walk out of her life right now and into one of her novels. What joy it would be to know that no matter what happened, things would turn out all right in the end!

Still, as nice as that daydream was, she had places to be. With her coffee sadly finished, she pulled her boots on, picked up her handbag and rucksack and headed out of her apartment.

Her flat might be owned by her parents but it was in one of the slightly seedier areas of London, convenient for the campus but not the safest place to walk alone at night. As such her front door had a deadbolt that had to be locked from the outside so she turned back to the door as she pulled it closed and locked it. She turned back to the stairwell only to find that it wasn't there any more. In fact the whole corridor was gone and she was looking at a country garden.

She turned back to where her front door should be but it too had gone. She looked down at the keys she still held in her hands, as if that was proof that she had in fact just locked the door as she remembered.

"Excuse me?"

Carrie spun around towards the voice. It was a young woman dressed in (she guessed) Victorian clothes. Was this fancy dress? Or Candid Camera perhaps?

"Can I help you?"

Carrie tried to remember how to speak.

"Where am I?" she asked, quickly becoming frightened. Had she lost her mind?

"You're in our garden in Helstone."

"Helstone?" she queried.

"That's right."

Carrie shook her head. Perfect! Bloody perfect! Somehow she was in the fictional village of Helstone which meant that either she was asleep, and she was pretty sure she remembered waking up and leaving the flat, or she was insane.

"Where did you expect to be?" The woman asked her.

"The last thing I remember, I was in London." There, that was truthful at least.

"And you have no idea how you got here?"

"Nope, not a one." Okay, that wasn't strictly true, she certainly suspected that she was hallucinating.

"Your clothes are very unusual," the girl noted. "Is that what you usually wear?"

Carrie looked down at her jeans and sweater. Of course they looked odd here, women had probably never even considered wearing trousers in the 1850s and whilst her clothes were not what might be called revealing in her time, they certainly were much more form fitting than a respectable young woman in this time might wear. Actually, they were probably more form fitting than even disreputable women in this time wore.

"No." There, keep the lies small and don't elaborate, that was something her mother had taught her.

"Are you perhaps injured?" the woman asked.

"I don't know," Carrie answered, because now that she thought about it, she could well have been hit on the head and right about now be lying in a coma somewhere. This could just be a coma dream, if there was such a thing.

"Well, let's get you inside."

"Who are you?" Carrie asked.

"My name is Margaret Hale." She smiled reassuringly at Carrie.

"Oh." Really, she should have been expecting that so she shouldn't be as shocked as she felt.

She suddenly remembered how people always thought Margaret haughty, and seeing her for herself she supposed she could understand why. Carrie was often accused of being standoffish but really it was because she was shy, not arrogant. She saw a lot of herself in Margaret, which was one of the reasons why she loved the book so much.

"And you are?" Margaret prompted.

"Oh, right, uh, I'm Carrie. I mean Caroline, Caroline Preston, but people call me Carrie."

"Pleased to meet you, Miss Preston." Margaret gave a slight bow so Carrie followed suit.

"And you."

"Well, let's get you inside. Perhaps you would like some tea?"

"Um..."

Margaret put her arm around Carrie's shoulder and guided her inside.

The house, or vicarage, Carrie corrected herself, had clearly seen better days. Some of the wallpaper was slightly faded and the rugs in the hallway were rather old and slightly threadbare in places. Still, the place was immaculate and the floors had been polished to within an inch of their lives. No, this wasn't a show house, rather it was a home, and all the more welcome for its signs of wear and tear.

Margaret left her in the study and Carrie had a few moments to think whilst Margaret set about ordering some tea and fetching her father. If this was a dream, she wondered how to wake up. She tried pinching herself but that didn't work so, remembering that Inception film she had watched recently, she tried jumping like they did to wake herself up, but alas that also didn't work.

She sat back down, feeling glad that no one had witnessed her jumping up and down like a mad woman, and turned her mind to a good excuse for being here. She really didn't think *'I was on my way to Uni in the 21st century when I suddenly ended up here'* would go down particularly well. The folks in this time hadn't even heard of Einstein yet, let alone his theories on time travel and parallel universes.

"How are you feeling?" Margaret asked as she returned a few moments later with a tray of tea and her father in tow.

"Um, rather disoriented to be honest."

"This is my father, Mr Hale. Father, this is Miss Preston," Margaret said as she put the tea tray down on the desk and set about pouring it.

"Very pleased to meet you, Miss Preston," Mr Hale said with a slight bow.

"And you, Mr Hale," she answered, returning his bow and thinking that these manners would take some getting used to.

"My daughter tells me that you are confused as to how you came to be here?"

"That's right. I was in London and the next thing I remember I was here."

"I'm afraid our village is too small to have a resident doctor but I am something of a learned man myself. Would it be all right if I examined you to see if you are hurt."

"Of course."

Mr Hale took her pulse, felt around her head for a lump then sat down beside her and asked a few more questions about how she came to be here, why she was dressed strangely and what she remembered.

"What of your family?" He asked when he had finished.

"I have no family. They..." She hated to tempt fate by saying this but really, what other excuse could she use? If she said they were alive, Mr Hale would surely insist on trying to contact them. "They're dead."

"You're an orphan?" Margaret asked, her voice full of compassion. She handed her a cup of tea which Carrie accepted with a smile.

"Thank you. I'm a bit old to be an called an orphan, but yes, I suppose I am."

"Well, drink your tea, Miss Preston, we will be back in a moment," Mr Hale said, rising and escorting Margaret out of the room. Carrie knew they were going to talk about her but there was little she could do to stop them. Instead she set her mind to ways to get home, or wake up, or whatever the hell it was that she needed to do to get out of this freak show!

Mr Hale and Margaret went next door to the sitting room where Mrs Hale was waiting for them. Not wanting to overwhelm the girl, Mr Hale had asked his wife to wait in her sitting room while they spoke with Carrie.

He filled his wife in on what had been said, on the girl's unusual dress, her memory loss and her seeming lack of injury.

"Why should she appear dressed so strangely?" Margaret asked.

"Perhaps she had no choice in her manner of dress," Mr Hale suggested. "Perhaps those were the only clothes she could find."

"So what do you think has happened to her?" Mrs

Hale asked, her voice grave, for anything that robbed a young woman of her clothing could not be a good thing.

"I do not know," Mr Hale began. "But I have read about a condition called amnesia, which is essentially memory loss. Sometimes this can happen after a head injury but sometimes something so awful can happen that a person literally forgets about it, unable to face the horror of their own memories."

"And you think that something awful has happened to Miss Preston?" Margaret said, her voice again full of compassion.

"She seems physically unharmed so I think it likely that she experienced or saw something terribly traumatic, and that is why she has no memory of how she came to be here."

"So what should we do?" Mrs Hale asked.

"We must take care of her," Margaret said. "Though her turn of phrase can be unusual, her accent is that of a lady and she is clearly not from the working classes. Since she has no family of her own, I believe it is our Christian duty to take her in and look after her."

"But we are leaving for Milton in six days!" Mrs Hale said, clearly still upset by that fact.

"I know, Mother, but I see no reason why Miss Preston cannot come with us, if she would like to."

"Margaret is right," Mr Hale agreed with his daughter. "I believe that there is a reason Miss Preston ended up in our garden, so that we might open our hearts to her and take her in."

Mrs Hale nodded, clearly not that happy with the idea but knowing that her husband was right and that they couldn't in all good conscience turn her away.

"Good," Margaret smiled. "I will take her upstairs and find something more appropriate for her to wear, then I shall ask if she would like to stay with us."

Mr Hale smiled warmly at his daughter. She really was a good girl.

After being in this fictional world for a week, Carrie was resigned to staying here for the foreseeable future and had decided that she might as well try to enjoy her time here. She did wonder if perhaps this was like Life On Mars and she was trapped in purgatory, but regardless of how she came to be here, she couldn't seem to find a way back to reality.

The hardest thing about being here was adjusting her speech. Back home Carrie was a polite and well-mannered girl but by Victorian standards she was rather uncouth and at times vulgar. She used a lot of abbreviations and some words which were considered harmless in her time were positively shocking here. When, for example, she had asked if the neighbours cat, Mrs Tiddles, was pregnant, Margaret had looked at her as if she'd just dropped the F bomb and muttered something about the cat expecting a litter. Mr Hale had blushed and hidden his face behind a book and Mrs Hale had looked as though she might pass out.

Carrie had mumbled something about it being a term she had read in a medical book and apologised, saying that she had not had any experience of such things personally.

Thankfully they accepted this and readily forgave her. She still felt like a fish out of water most of the time but the Hales were extremely kind to her and usually put her faux pas down to her 'trauma'. She had an inkling of what they thought this trauma might be but they never pressed her to remember, probably believing it best that she retain her amnesia of any 'horrific events'.

It surprised Carrie how readily they accepted her as a member of the family. She didn't call Mr and Mrs Hale Mum and Dad, obviously, but she was treated exactly the same as Margaret and afforded every courtesy that their daughter received. Carrie could tell that Mrs Hale found this slightly more difficult than her husband but she also felt that in a way, her being here was helping Mrs Hale as it provided her with a distraction. It was clear for anyone with eyes to see that Mrs Hale was dreading the move to Milton and so Carrie willingly became Mrs Hale's and Dixon's doll as they set about sorting through Mrs Hale's wardrobe to find clothes that were suitable for Carrie. Dixon said that she was able to alter a few of the outfits to keep them fashionable but on the whole, Mrs Hales clothes just weren't suitable for a young woman and Carrie mostly shared Margaret's wardrobe.

Mrs Hale often lamented that money would soon be so tight that they could not afford to buy Carrrie her own clothes. Carrie assured her that the kindness she had already been shown was far too generous as it was, whilst Margaret assured her mother that, thanks to spending much of her time in London with her rich aunt, Mrs Shaw, she had many more dresses than she needed and was more than happy to share them with Carrie.

Now though, as they headed to Milton on the train, Mrs Hale and Dixon were not with them. Mr Hale and Margaret thought it best if they went to the seaside for two weeks while Mr Hale, Margaret and Carrie set about moving into the new home in Milton.

Carrie felt that the move was a good thing, since it occupied her mind and kept her from growing too fretful that she seemed to be stuck here. She knew that Mr and Miss Hale had both met Mr Thornton when they came up to Milton for a day to secure a house for them and as they sat on the train, Carrie passed the time by asking a lot of questions about both him and Milton. She also knew from the book that Margaret had not made a very favourable first impression on Mr Thornton but there was little she could do to change that at the moment.

Still, Carrie was looking forward to watching their romance unfold before her eyes.

"He really is quite a taciturn sort of man," Margaret told Carrie of her first impression of Mr Thornton.

"Perhaps, but maybe he was intimidated by meeting you?" Carrie suggested. "I doubt he meets many ladies. Don't think too badly of him."

Margaret wasn't sure what to say to that. She knew nothing of trade or manufacturing so she was content not to think of Mr Thornton at all, for he was neither of her class nor was he her equal.

The biggest surprise that Milton held for Carrie was the air. People in her time spoke of pollution but really, they hadn't a clue what they were talking about. The air here looked perpetually misty as a thin veil of smoke hung in the air. The buildings were all filthy, covered in what looked like decades of grime but, in some cases at least, was probably only a few years of smoke and soot.

One thing she did find pleasant though, was the scent of the smoke. It wasn't particularly strong but it reminded her of the fires that her Aunt Imm used to have in her home. Her parents preferred central heating but Imm liked to hear the crackle of the wood and the glow from the coal that only came from a real fire. She and Aunt Imm spent many nights in front of the fire, drinking cocoa, playing board games or sometimes snuggling up under a duvet to watch films.

They settled into the house within a week, managing to unpack within two days and spending the rest of their days fine-tuning the house; cleaning until it gleamed, finding just the right spot for furnishings, the right throws, covers and cushions for the chairs and rearranging the ornaments until they were satisfied with the displays.

Carrie smiled when Margaret seemed pleased by the change in wallpapers when they first arrived, for Margaret didn't know that it was Mr Thornton who had persuaded the landlord to change his mind and redecorate for his new tenants.

When Mr Thornton arrived for his first lesson with Mr Hale, Carrie opened the door to him, eager to finally meet the man that she had dreamed about for so many years. She found herself struck dumb as she opened the door, for he was quite the most striking man she had seen in a long time. Elizabeth Gaskell had been been rather harsh when she called his features unremarkable, for to Carrie he looked rather like a Calvin Kline model might have. His eyes were light blue and accentuated by the dark lashes that framed them and his jaw was strong and square. Yes, in her time at least, there was nothing at all unremarkable about this man and she couldn't help but wonder what he might look like modelling a pair of Calvin Kline's. Just Calvin Kline's, that is.

"Mr Thornton?" she asked, finally finding her voice, though it was a shade or two huskier than her normal voice.

Chapter Two

Mr Thornton removed his hat and seemed to shake himself out of a stupor a moment or two after she had spoken his name. He wondered who this girl was. He knew that Mr Hale only had one daughter whom he had already met, yet this girl didn't look like a servant for her dress, while simple, was much too fine to be that of a servant. Unless perhaps she was a lady's maid, though from what Mr Thornton knew of their finances, one would hardly expect the Hales to be able to afford a lady's maid, nor indeed would most lady's maids consent to answer the door like a common housemaid.

"Indeed," he smiled. "Though I'm afraid you have me at something of a disadvantage."

"Oh, yes. I'm Carrie Preston," she held her hand out to him. "Pleased to meet you."

Mr Thornton looked shocked that she was so forward but he shook her hand nonetheless.

"Please, come in." Carrie stood aside and Mr Thornton entered, pulling his gloves off and stowing them in his pocket.

She closed the door then took his hat and coat from him.

"How are you settling in?" Mr Thornton asked as she turned her back to him for a moment to hang his coat up.

"Oh, very well, thank you." She turned back to face him and lowered her voice. "And thank you for getting the wallpaper changed. Though I didn't see it, the description of the old paper alone was enough to make me shudder."

"I'm sorry, I don't-"

"Come, Mr Thornton, I hardly think the landlord

24

relented because he wanted to impress Mr Hale."

Mr Thornton smiled. He had asked the landlord not to say anything because he didn't want the Hales to feel indebted to him but nevertheless, it was always nice when one's efforts were appreciated.

"I haven't said anything to the family," she assured him, finding his modesty rather endearing.

"Thank you."

Carrie smiled back.

"This way," she said, leading him to Mr Hale's study. As she closed the door behind him and found herself alone in the hallway she bit her lip to keep from squealing but she couldn't stop the ear to ear grin that formed on her lips.

She had just met Mr John Thornton, manufacturer, magistrate and frequent star of her racier daydreams. She wasn't disappointed.

Mr Thornton, however, was disappointed that Miss Preston had left since he had hoped to be able to spend a little more time with her. Not only was she very handsome, she was obviously insightful and he was intrigued by her, to say the least.

"Ah, Mr Thornton, how good to see you. Do sit down," Mr Hale greeted him.

They exchanged pleasantries and Mr Thornton took a seat.

"Carrie has offered to bring us up some tea in a few minutes."

"She is your servant then?" he asked, for she certainly had not looked like a servant.

"Oh no, she is my ward but she does like to make herself useful. Our maid is with my wife at the seaside. This move has troubled her greatly and I thought it would be easier on her if we moved whilst she and Dixon took a little break and some sea air. Carrie has been a marvel, making sure

Margaret and I are properly fed and watered."

"I hope you do not mind me asking, but how did she come to be in your care?"

"Well, it's something of a mystery, as a matter of fact. Margaret found her in our garden with no memory of how she got from London to Helstone."

"She does not have family of her own?"

"No, I understand they are deceased. She is rather vague on the matter but I gather that they perished in a house fire."

"I'm sorry to hear that. You and your wife took her in?"

"Well, what else could we do? It seemed clear to me that she had suffered some form of trauma that had left her with amnesia, she had no other family to take care of her and it is very unseemly for a young woman to live on her own. We couldn't, in all good conscience, turn her away."

"No, of course not."

John had many other things he wanted to ask but it would be impolite to be too inquisitive.

"So, have you given any thought to which book you would like to start with?" Mr Hale asked him.

Just then the door opened and Carrie came in with a tea tray which she placed on the table and began serving from. He watched her as she poured the tea and he was fascinated to see that she bit down gently on her lip from time to time as she concentrated on her task. She handed him the cup and his finger touched hers. He saw her eyes meet his and he wondered if she had just felt the same swell of emotion that he had at that simple touch. She swallowed and withdrew her hand.

As she prepared Mr Hale's tea she seemed slightly flustered and that pleased him, for it meant that she too had felt something. She handed Mr

Hale his tea and quickly left, almost scurrying out of the room. She struck him as somewhat shy and introverted, though it seemed that she tried to hide those tendencies.

Of course he had very little to base those beliefs on but he was rather astute when it came to reading someone's character so he very much doubted that he was wrong.

Finally he returned his full attention to Mr Hale, only to discover that he had evidently agreed to start his lessons with Homer. Thankfully Mr Hale seemed blissfully ignorant of Mr Thornton's interest in his ward.

Mr Thornton focused on the lesson for the rest of the hour and stayed well beyond his time, hopeful that Carrie would put in a further appearance but she did not. Finally he left, though he thought that Mr Hale seemed disappointed to see him go.

He hoped that he might see Carrie on his way out but alas it was not to be. Still, there would be many more lessons and, he hoped, many more chances to see her.

Chapter Three

Mrs Hale and Dixon joined them a few days later, looking quite happy after their holiday but within two weeks of arriving in Milton, both women had come down with a dreadful cold. Though not a medical woman, Carrie was something of a geek and as such her mind was a positive trove of useless information. She knew that there was no such thing as paracetamol or aspirin in these times but she also knew that both drugs could be found in tree bark and that before they had been distilled into pure drugs, they were a herbal remedy.

She had been given an allowance by Mr Hale, which really was too kind of him given how little money the family had, but after he refused her protests she accepted it gracefully, for to continue to refuse would have been rude. Now she was glad of it as it would allow her to buy the tree bark for Mrs Hale.

Unwilling to spend any money on her own dresses, she was still wearing Margaret's clothes. Fortunately Margaret didn't seem to mind sharing her wardrobe, though Carrie was careful to keep away from the few dresses Margaret expressed a preference for.

Unfortunately her size seven feet were far larger than Margaret's and Carrie only possessed one pair of boots, those that she had been wearing when she arrived here. Thankfully they were her day boots which she wore to class, so they were relatively comfortable with only a small heel.

She was also keen to help Dixon out around the house, though she had to say that housework in the 1850s was much harder than housework in 2011.

Oh, what she wouldn't give for her washing machine and tumble drier right about now!

Some tasks weren't so bad though. This morning for example she had helped Dixon to make shampoo and conditioner. Dixon didn't see the point in using conditioner but Carrie had been insistent and as a lady's maid, Dixon had plenty of recipes that she could chose from.

The shampoo could be made in bulk since it was made using chamomile, soap flakes and glycerine. The conditioner was harder to keep since it required fresh egg yoke so whilst Carrie insisted upon washing her hair twice a week, she only used the conditioner once a week. Carrie hated rinsing her hair with cold water but she had little choice unless she wanted scrambled-egg-hair. Still, the recipe Dixon had for dry hair conditioner also used jojoba, almond and calendula oil and left her hair feeling beautifully soft after the harsh shampoo, so it was worth a weekly dousing in cold water.

There was little about bathing in this time that Carrie enjoyed. Baths were taken only once a week, on a Saturday night and were nothing like the baths that Carrie was used it. It simply consisted of a small copper tub that would be dragged out into the kitchen and filled with hot water from the stove. Each family member would then stand in the tub and wash themselves. Not only was the idea of bathing in someone else's water rather icky, Carrie saw no point in simply standing in a large bowl of water. Sure, it was easier to scoop over herself but it was also easy to spill said water all over the floor.

After trying that once, Carrie had insisted on a daily wash and when it was her turn to bathe, she shooed Dixon out of the room and, kneeling beside the tub, only used it to shampoo and rinse her hair.

The water was warm though so she had to rinse her conditioner out over the sink using cold water from the well.

Dixon was also rather shocked that Carrie liked to wash her hair twice a week. At home it would have been every other day but she was content to compromise here and wash it every third day. Still, it was something of a hassle to do with just her small wash basin and water jug.

What she wouldn't give for hot and cold running water right about now. Or even her power shower. Oh, to think that's he had ever taken such things for granted!

Now, she was tasked with restocking their supply of almond oil and chamomile tea, since they had used them all in the shampoo that morning. She had already been to the two shops where Dixon told her that they might be purchased and with those tasks out of the way, she stopped an elderly gentleman as he passed her.

"Excuse me, sir, I wonder if you can help me. I am new to Milton and I am looking for a chemist shop."

"Pardon me, a what?"

"Oh, um, an apothecary or a herbal remedy shop." She had no idea what they were called in this day and age.

"Ah," he smiled. "There is an apothecary on Chambers Street. Do you know where that is?"

"I think so, I've looked at a map of Milton. Thank you."

He touched his hat, bid her good day and walked away. Carrie made her way towards where she believed Chambers Street could be found.

She couldn't remember which bark asprin was found in so she asked the man behind the counter for something to reduce a fever. He offered her powered cinchona bush bark, which she knew contained paracetamol, or powered willow bark, which she now remembered was the one with aspirin in. Knowing that paracetamol was the more dangerous of the two drugs in large amounts, she opted for willow bark. The last thing she wanted was to give Mrs Hale liver failure since she didn't know how much of the drug was in any given amount.

The shopkeeper advised her how much of the powered willow bark to administer and after weighing the powder, he poured it into a small bottle, which he placed a cork stopper into before he handed it to her.

She paid for it and left the shop, only to see Mr Thornton heading towards her.

Even after only one meeting, her feelings for him were so strong that she had chosen to avoid him at his last two lessons, preferring to let Dixon or Margaret open the door to him. It had taken all her willpower to remain in the kitchen while he was in the house and not even peek at him as he arrived and left, but somehow she had managed it.

Her heart skipped a beat and she found herself quite stupefied for a moment as she watched him approach, though thankfully by the time he reached her, she had regained some of her sense. She bowed slightly to him.

"Mr Thornton, how good to see you again."

"Miss Preston." He looked to the shop she had just exited. "I hope you are not unwell?"

"Oh, no. Mrs Hale has a dreadful cold though and I thought some willow bark would help her fever."

"I am sorry to hear that."

They fell into step beside one another.

"What brings you into town?" Carrie asked.

"Oh, I have come from the cotton exchange."

"I hope business was good this morning." She said, doing her best to make polite conversation, for this man really did turn her into a simpleton when she was in his presence.

"Quite good, thank you."

"Good." She smiled and cast her mind around for another topic of conversation. "Um, I have been thinking recently about getting a job and I thought that you might be the person to ask."

"You want to work?" He sounded stunned.

"I do. The Hales have been very good to me but I really would rather pay my own way, I would like to give them something in the way of housekeeping for looking after me, and I feel just awful taking money off them when they don't have a lot."

"Excuse me, I was under the impression that ladies from the south didn't work."

"Believe me, my mother and sister agree with you." Her smile faded. "Agreed with you," she corrected. They may not have been close but Carrie was starting to miss her family as well as her friends.

"I'm sorry," Mr Thornton said, catching the change in tense and how her voice turned sad.

"Anyway," she rushed on, preferring not to dwell on sad thoughts. "I am of a different mind and like to be independent. I'm not skilled at anything but I can read and write; I pick new things up quickly and I'm willing to turn my hand to anything, even factory work."

"Nay!" he looked appalled by the idea. "A fine young lady like yourself is not made for the likes of mill work."

"Beggars can't be choosers," she smiled. "But if

you could keep your ear open for anything that might be suitable, I would appreciate it."

"Of course," he said. "What did you have in mind, something like a governess?"

"Oh, God no! I worked as a au pair once; dreadful job."

"A what?"

"Oh, a nanny. I'm sorry, my family spent many years abroad so I have some strange language at times." Which was true, she had lived in Spain for five years when she was young. In fact her father still lived out there.

"So what did you have in mind?" he asked her.

"I don't know, office work? Administration? I'm not bad at maths so perhaps even book keeping or shop work. But like I said, I'm willing to try anything, even mill work."

"Give me a few days," he said. "Don't do anything hasty."

"Oh please, procrastination could be my middle name." She winked at him.

Mr Thornton frowned, not at her words, though he did not like the idea of her getting a job, but at her wink! Young ladies did not wink. Well, the ones he knew didn't. They also didn't want jobs and think it was their duty to contribute to the household in any way other than living in it, or sometimes running it.

Granted, his mother was freer with her attitude; she had often helped him with matters of business, but then she would freely admit she was a tradesman's wife and a manufacturers mother, not a lady.

Of course, in working class families, the daughters were expected to work as soon as they were able, just as the sons were. It wasn't a woman working that he found so strange, it was this woman wanting to work.

"Well," she said, pulling him out of his thoughts, "I should get this home. I don't want to leave Mrs Hale in distress for any longer than necessary."

"Of course. Good day, Miss Preston."

"Good day, Mr Thornton," she said with a somewhat theatrical bow and a cheeky smile, for the overly formal manners of this society still amused her. She wondered what Mr Thornton would say if she just left him with a jaunty wave and a 'bye' or 'see ya'.

Mr Thornton couldn't be sure but he thought that she found his manner amusing. In almost every way she was lady, yet she was willing to flout convention by winking at him, now she seemed to make fun of him for adopting the manners of a gentleman. She really was a puzzle. She infuriated him and pleased him in equal measure and more than that, she captivated him because as yet he didn't know how or why she behaved as she did. She was a puzzle, and one he fully intended to solve.

A few days later Mr Thornton had been invited to tea with the Hales. His mother had almost laughed at the notion that he should dress to take tea with them but however low they had been brought, they were still gentry and they deserved his respect. He also couldn't help thinking that he wanted to look his best for Miss Preston, though he had tried not to dwell on such thoughts.

His mother seemed offended by the haughty way in which Mrs and Miss Hale had treated her and John's sister, Fanny, when they called, and indeed Mr Thornton had observed that behaviour for himself when he had first met Miss Hale. It was strange though, because whilst his mother didn't want John marrying Miss Hale, she seemed rather affronted that Miss Hale didn't seem interested in her son.

Thankfully Miss Preston hadn't been present when she had called on the Hales and as such his mother hadn't passed judgement on her yet.

"I was thinking that I might take someone else on in the office," he had casually said to his mother before he left that evening. "There has been a backlog building up that I never quite get around to clearing."

"Can we afford it?" she asked.

"I was thinking I might hire a woman, perhaps just part-time, at least in the beginning."

Knowing that women's wages were usually half that of a man, this appeased Mrs Thornton.

"Very well, just make sure you choose someone with a brain in her head rather than a pretty face."

"What if I find someone with both?" John teased.

"Get on with you, foolish boy." Mrs Thornton scowled, though John could see she was just playing.

He bent down and kissed her cheek.

"Don't wait up."

He was hoping he would get a chance to speak with Carrie this evening, to tell her that he had secured work for her. He wondered how she would react. Would she be pleased as he hoped, or were her words the other day only a veiled attempt at garnering sympathy and possibly get money from him. He didn't like to doubt Miss Preston but he couldn't help but remember how his sister often angled indirectly for money if she had spent all of her allowance.

Thankfully Carrie opened the door to him and he had his opportunity to speak with her.

"Mr Thornton, how lovely to see you again."

"Miss Preston." He stepped inside and Carrie took his hat and coat from him, which she hung up by the door. "I was hoping I might get a chance to speak with you alone."

"Oh?" she turned to him, looking puzzled and slightly apprehensive.

His spirits plummeted as he realised she hadn't been serious about finding work. Nonetheless, he had done as she asked and he would finish what he intended to say.

"I believe I have found you employment as a clerk, of sorts."

"Oh? Oh!" Her confused frown was replaced with a broad smile. When he had said he wanted to speak to her 'alone', her first thought had been that he might like her and while she would dearly love for Mr Thornton to fall in love with her she was, needless to say, a little worried that she would mess up her favourite romance.

"That's wonderful news," she smiled. "Thank you so much. I have been looking through the papers every day but the only positions I have found for a woman have been living-in as a governess, and you know my feelings about that line of work."

"It's my pleasure," he said, relaxing, for whatever had caused her discomfort earlier, her smile seemed genuine now. "I wasn't sure if you had said anything to the Hales yet so I though it best to speak to you in private."

"No, I haven't said anything yet in case they object."

"Come by the mill about ten tomorrow morning and I'll go through the details with you."

On impulse she stretched up on her toes and kissed his cheek. She knew that the job might be unsuitable but right now she didn't care. He had helped her and she was grateful.

Mr Thornton watched as she almost skipped off down the hall. Her lips seemed to have warmed his flesh where she had kissed his cheek and he found himself unable to follow her for a moment. That was very forward of her, no doubt, and very unladylike indeed but it had been so heartfelt, not to mention welcome, that he couldn't think ill of her for it. She turned back to him as she reached the bottom of the stairs, her eyes asking whether he was coming or not.

He rediscovered the ability to walk and followed her up the stairs to the parlour.

After the greetings were done with and everyone had taken a seat, Dixon brought a tea tray in. Carrie smiled as Mr Thornton watched Margaret while she served the tea, seemingly fascinated with the bracelet that kept falling down her arm as she poured.

'This is it!' Carrie thought. *'He's falling in love.'*

Mr Hale and Mr Thornton began discussing the power loom and Carrie listened with interest. The mechanism used to separate the threads was ingenious and the idea of using heedles and heedle bars to separate and lift different strands of the weft was so simple, yet something she would probably never have thought of herself in a million years.

"Fascinating," she said softly, causing both men to turn and look at her. "Don't you think, Margaret?" she asked the other woman, embarrassed to have spoken aloud and drawn their attention.

"Sorry? Oh yes, very interesting," Margaret said. Clearly she hadn't been paying much attention to the conversation, though she did rise to refill the tea cups.

Carrie was feeling quite put out with Margaret. No wonder it took her so long to like Mr Thornton, because she was so bloody indifferent to him that she didn't have a chance to get to know him. Still, Mr Thornton seemed smitten, watching with interest while her father used Margaret's index finger and thumb as sugar tongs.

She felt a pang of jealousy, until he looked in her direction and smiled warmly at her. A moment later she felt a pang of dread. What if he liked her more than Margaret?

She forced herself to smile back. He was just being polite, that's all. Margaret was the one for him, there was no doubt in her mind.

"Margaret has recently started embroidering a lovely piece of cambric for her cousin Edith's baby," Carrie said, trying to induce Margaret to join the conversation. "It is lovely work but I dare say she wouldn't mind technology like your loom to make it easier for her,"

"Nonsense," Margaret chimed in. "It is the very fact that it is handmade which makes it so special. Were it mass produced on a machine, it would not be made with nearly the same care and attention to detail."

Catching Mr Thornton's rather offended look following Margaret's words, Carrie decided that perhaps she was better off keeping her mouth shut.

"I'm sure it's lovely," Mr Thornton told Margaret, managing to keep a civil tongue in his head.

"Yes, well," Mr Hale seemed to have picked up on the insult even if Margaret still looked blissfully oblivious to the offence she had caused. He swiftly moved the conversation on so Carrie picked up some knitting and set about completing it. She wasn't very good, Mrs Hale had only taught her a few weeks ago but at least mistakes she made could be unpicked so she wasn't wasting materials. She kept her eyes focused intently on her work, even if she couldn't help her ears listening to Mr Thornton's conversation.

She felt his eyes on her occasionally and the one time she was unable to resist glancing up, the look she saw on his face quite made her shiver with desire. Mark had never made her feel like that, she thought, hastily averting her eyes and squeezing her thighs together to ease some of the tension she felt.

She listened as Margaret defended the south, listened as Mr Thornton explained about his childhood, his father dying and finding himself head of the family at only sixteen years of age. Finally Carrie was unable to remain focused on her knitting so she put the work aside and looked up at him. He was matter of fact about his past, asking not for pity or sympathy but simply claiming his due as a self-made man. She smiled at him, wanting him to know that she liked him for his honesty.

Finally he rose to leave, shaking hands with Mr Hale, Mrs Hale and Carrie but when he made the same gesture to Margaret she was not expecting it and bowed instead. Thinking that he had been snubbed, Mr Thornton's features clouded once again and he left. Fearing his anger, Carrie followed him.

"Please," she said as he stopped by the front door to put his coat on. "Don't think badly of Margaret, she's not used to shaking hands with people and she wasn't prepared for it. She didn't mean any offence."

"And yet that seems to be all she causes."

"Mr Thornton, I know that Margaret can appear haughty but she is not, really, she's just not used to your ways up here. Underneath that somewhat imposing exterior is a heart of gold and she will be very upset at the thought that she's offended you."

"Tell me, Miss Preston, you are also from the south, are you not?"

"Yes, I was born in London."

"And until now, have you spent any time in the north?"

"Um," she was rather confused by this line of questioning. "I went skiing in Aviemore once, in Scotland."

"Skiing?"

"Yes, it's a kind of sport."

"Yes, well, Scotland may be to the north but it is its own country. You have never been to the north of England before then?"

"No, I don't think so."

"So you are a southerner who has no experience of the north and yet you have adapted to our ways with relative ease."

"No, I..." Oh dear, this was not going well. "I've spent a lot of time abroad so I'm used to different cultures but Margaret has been rather sheltered."

Mr Thornton was starting to look angry again, but this time with Carrie.

"Miss Preston, you can defend Miss Hale until the cows come home but I speak as I find and so far I find her to be of a most disagreeable disposition."

He put his hat on his head, opened the front door and walked out. To her relief he paused and turned back.

"Good evening," he said graciously, all traces of anger gone from his voice.

"Good night, Mr Thornton." She smiled, pleased that she seemed to have been forgiven.

She closed the door behind him and with a sigh,

returned to the sitting room. She arrived just in time to hear Margaret say "Papa, I do think Mr. Thornton a very remarkable man; but personally I do not like him at all."

"You don't know him at all," Carrie snapped at her.

"And you do?" Margaret asked.

"Yes! Not well, obviously, at least not yet but I can see beyond the tradesman to the fair and just man underneath and if you can't, then you are letting your prejudices show."

"That is hardly fair," Margaret complained.

"Maybe not," Carrie agreed. "But no less fair than you judging him without getting to know him first."

All of the Hales were staring at her and she blushed.

"I'm sorry," Carrie sighed. "I shouldn't have said that. I think I'll go to bed now, it's been a long day."

She bid them goodnight and headed up to her bedroom, hoping that she had not just alienated them by being rude to their daughter. Mr Hale would understand, wouldn't he?

Chapter Four

The next morning Carrie was eager to apologise to Margaret at the first opportunity, which thankfully came early as they shared a room and awoke around the same time.

"Margaret, I'm sorry about what I said last night."

"Don't be," Margaret said. "My father informs me that you were right."

"I'm sure you'd like Mr Thornton, if only you gave him a chance."

"It will not be easy," Margaret said with a sigh. "Manufacturing is a rough business and his stance of being at war with his workers is one that I simply cannot agree with but as I said to father, I will try to be more understanding at future meetings."

That was enough for Carrie, at least for now and she set about her morning routine.

Her toothbrush was made from a bone handle with badger hair bristles and her toothpaste was a mixture of bicarbonate of soda and chalk. It tasted foul but she supposed it did the job. Thankfully she had managed to acquire a little peppermint oil and before dabbing her brush in the powder, she added a few drops of oil to the bristles. It was no Colgate but it was better than nothing.

After she had dressed, Dixon put her hair up for her then Carrie headed down to breakfast and chatted with Mr and Mrs Hale until Margaret joined them. She did not tell them she was seeing Mr Thornton about a job today because she felt it was better to present it to them as a done deal. She also did not want to jinx herself because whatever this job was, she didn't have it yet.

When Mr Hale asked what their plans for the day

were, Margaret informed him she was going to see Bessy, the young girl she had met from Princeton. Carrie told him that she was planning to take a walk and hoping to explore some new areas of the town.

Before she left, she went back up to her room and pulled her handbag out from under her bed. She had not worn makeup since she had arrived here but today she felt that she needed a little additional courage. She dabbed a little concealer under her eyes, patted her complexion down with powder and added just a tiny bit of mascara to her eyelashes. Makeup was not common here and if she wore too much, she would stick out like a clown in a church.

She got her jewellery out of her purse and considered wearing it since it also gave her courage. She had noticed however, that gemstones were not common in this time and diamonds especially. So she left her solitaire earrings, ring and pendant in her purse and put on only the small amethyst earrings that her aunt had left her. She did slip her artificial diamond horse brooch into her purse though, so that it was with her even if she couldn't wear it. It was her good luck charm.

When she had remembered her aunt's words about the earrings, it had occurred to her that they might be responsible for this freaky situation she now found herself in and she had removed them immediately in the hopes that she might return to her time. It hadn't worked and though she had many theories as to why she was trapped in this fictional world, she still had no answers.

Finally ready, she put her makeup away in her handbag and slipped it back under her bed, alongside her rucksack that housed her Uni books and laptop.

She began humming to herself as she walked to

the mill, for music always calmed her. She missed her CD player. Her mobile phone had some music on and she did have headphones for it, but she knew she would quickly wear the battery down if she used it much so she settled for humming. Perhaps one day she could afford a piano, then she could play all her favourite music.

As she approached the mill she grew nervous and she paused outside to wipe her damp palms on her skirt.

"Wish me luck," she said softly to her aunt, looking to the heavens. Then she took a deep breath, mustering as much courage as she could and strode through the mill yard and into the offices.

Mr Thornton's door was open and as he heard her enter, he came through to greet her ushering her into his office and closing the door behind them.

"How are you?" he asked.

"I'm fine, thank you. I hope you're not still upset about last night?"

"I am not," he confirmed. "But I should not have been sharp with you, it was not you that I was upset with."

Knowing that he hadn't liked it when she defended Margaret last night, Carrie didn't try again and let the matter drop. Mr Thornton gestured to the chair opposite his desk and Carrie sat down.

"So, Mr Thornton, what's this job you have heard about?"

"Actually you would be working for me."

"For you?" She hadn't counted on that.

"Is that a problem?" he asked, sounding hurt at her surprise.

"No, not at all. I'm just... well I am a little surprised that you require someone. I had been led to believe that your mill was one of the most efficient in the town." Okay, that wasn't strictly true but she had to cover her surprise somehow. The truth was that she was already madly in love with Mr Thornton and working with him every day would be torture.

"We are, but I find that the office work is running behind in some areas. It would be helpful to have someone to do the tasks I haven't found the time to do."

"Of course," she smiled. "What kind of tasks did you have in mind?"

He got up and showed her piles of paper work that were sitting on various filing cabinets and tables.

"These are paid invoices, these are unpaid, these are correspondence, these are tenders awaiting replies, these are potential orders awaiting a bid. These are receipts for supplies and deliveries, these are filled orders, these are unfilled orders and these are correspondence from various sources that need replying to but that I haven't had a chance yet. As you can see while there's a basic order, it still takes me a while to find things because I haven't had a chance to organise it."

Carrie thought she could handle that.

"The rest will be on an ad hoc basis,"he continued. "You'll be an assistant to me rather than a clerk, so I might ask you to do anything from running to the bank to signing for a delivery or taking the letters to the post office."

"I think that's within my capabilities," she smiled.

"Good," he smiled back and went to sit down at his desk. "Now, down to details. As to hours, I was thinking nine until two every day and a wage of eight shillings a week."

"Eight shillings?" she sounded incredulous.

"You were hoping for more?" His tone was hard.

"No. Eight shillings is twenty pounds a year for only five hours work a day! It's far too much."

Mr Thornton relaxed slightly.

"I believe a clerk working full-time would be paid in the region of fifty pounds for such duties."

"A man perhaps, but I am working half that time and I am a woman."

"I believe that to be a fair wage for the job," he said, though he knew it was higher than she would be paid anywhere else. Still, if she was competent and capable, he saw no reason not to pay her the same as a man.

"That's very generous of you," she said, desperately trying to find a way not to offend him with her next words. "However I would like to make it clear that when I asked for your help, I wasn't looking for a handout."

"Nor am I offering one."

"Good, because I am not a charity case and while I think you are a very generous and kind man, Mr Thornton, I have no desire to be in your debt."

"You won't be," he assured her. "As I said, that is a fair wage for the job."

Carrie stared at him for a few moments, trying to gauge how truthful he was but his features were inscrutable.

"Remind me not to play poker with you," she said, slightly irked by her inability to read him.

Mr Thornton smiled.

"Do we have a deal?" he asked her.

Carrie nodded then stood up and held her hand out.

"We do."

Mr Thornton shook her hand and relished the contact, however brief. He held on for a moment longer than was acceptable but finally he felt he had no choice but to release her.

"So, when do I start?" she asked.

"As soon as you'd like; the work is just piling up."

"I'll start now then."

And just like that she got to work. She cleared the boxes off a table in the corner, dragged the chair over to it and set about sorting the various papers.

She soon discovered that the filing cabinets were unused for a reason, because they were full. She began sorting the older documents for storage in boxes. Any paperwork that was over three years old was going into storage, though she labelled each box well so that things should be easy to find if they ever were needed. Finally having freed up some space, she began to organise the piles of paper, first into those that had been dealt with and those that hadn't. Those that needed attention she made into new pile, the other papers she arranged alphabetically to be filed away.

Mr Thornton tried to get on with his work and for the most part he was successful but every now and again he would look up to see her industriously sorting his office out and a smile would play at his lips. Absorbed in her work, she never looked over at him so he took the opportunity to examine her for a while.

She was an odd looking girl by nineteenth century standards of beauty but to him she looked perfect. Her features were strong rather than delicate, but as each was so perfect in his eyes, he found that strength only highlighted her beauty rather than detracted from it. Her hair was a very light shade of chestnut and her eyes were a bright emerald green.

He was annoyed when he was pulled from his contemplation by Williams knocking and informing him that he was needed on the floor. Mr Thornton followed him over to the mill as Williams explained that one of the looms had broken down. They arrived at the machine to see that the tuner was already repairing it and he told Mr Thornton that it was an easy repair and should take half an hour to fix. Satisfied, John left him to it and returned to his office but as he opened the door he heard Carrie utter a word no lady should even understand, let alone use.

"Oh bollocks!" she exclaimed as she began searching through her piles of paper.

Though he should have been offended, he found that the sound of such an elegant creature uttering such a profanity was immensely funny and burst out laughing.

"What?" she asked, turning to him.

"Nothing, just your colourful language. I take it you don't speak like that around Mr Hale?"

Carrie blushed a deep red. She had been trying so hard to remember the rules of this society but since she thought she was alone, her guard had dropped and it had just slipped out.

"Sorry. Sometimes I say things I don't mean."

"Don't apologise, I find it rather endearing. Though I am curious about where you learnt such a vulgar term."

"In Spain. It was quite a common curse out there." Poor old Spain had become the excuse for anything that she couldn't readily explain.

"This Spain you speak of sounds like a very unusual place. Nothing at all like my sister describes."

Damn, how could she have forgotten that his

48

sister liked The Tales of the Alhambra?

"Yes, well they don't put things like that in books, do they?"

Mr Thornton thought he detected a lie but he couldn't be sure.

"No, of course not," he agreed.

Carrie returned to her work and nothing more was said about it. The day wore on and Carrie kept working. John kept expecting her to need a break and when the lunch whistle rang, he was certain that she would want lunch, but the only thing she asked for all day was where she could get some water.

Finally at 3pm he drew her attention to the fact that her five hours were up for today.

"Oh," she seemed surprised, and maybe a little reluctant to finish her task. "I was on a roll," she said.

"A what?"

"Oh, um, I suppose it's when you've mastered a task and are moving along at a good rate and if you're interrupted it takes you a little while to get back up to full speed."

"Nevertheless, I can't have Mr Hale accusing me of overworking you, can I?"

"Oh, heaven forbid!" she teased.

"You will tell him, won't you? I don't want to keep secrets from him."

"Of course I'll tell him, I intend to start paying rent, or room and board, whatever it's called, and I expect he'll be a little curious as to where I'm getting my money from."

"Good. Then I'll see you tomorrow."

"Nine o'clock sharp, boss!" She put her shawl on ready to leave but remembered something. "Oh, I'll need some stationary supplies as well, files, dividers that kind of thing. How can I get those?"

John got up and went to the safe, opening it.

"There's a stationers on Mabel Lane." He handed her a note. "They open at nine so stop in before you come here."

Carrie was gradually getting used to the pricing here and had a fair idea what things were worth, but some objects were (relatively) much more expensive than they would have been in her time, and paper could well have been one of those things, so although she suspected that he had given her far too much, she couldn't be sure so she took the note and folded it into her small purse.

"I'll get receipts, of course," she assured him.

He had meant to tell her that and once again he was forced to wonder how a lady had any idea that receipts were necessary for all business expenses. He supposed that she might have gained that knowledge whilst learning how to run a household from her mother, but he suspected that wasn't the case.

"Have you worked before?" he asked, because really she had taken to her task with far too much ease.

"Every summer since I was sixteen," she smiled. She chose not to mention that she also worked two nights a week in a bar just off campus. She thought that kind of work would be frowned upon in these times.

"Why summers?" he asked.

"It's when I was off school," she said before she realised that women in these times didn't go to school, they had governesses who taught them at home. "I mean, that's when my brother was off school, we usually worked together so that he could keep his eye on me."

"Was your father in trade?" he asked, for surely

no gentleman would allow his daughter, or son for that matter, to work during the summer holidays.

"I suppose," she hedged, needing a moment to decide how much to tell him.

Officially her father was a Spanish Duke. Aged just ten years old, Carrie's grandmother had fled Spain with her parents, who had been vocal supporters of the recently ousted King, Alfonso XIII. As their only surviving child, she had inherited the title and Carrie's father had then inherited the title upon her death. Despite his ancestry however, he had no land or estate to go with his title and all his wealth had been earned by him and his English father.

The title didn't mean anything to Carrie and she always hated it when her mother insisted on people calling her 'Lady Preston', especially since it was only her title by marriage. Besides, Carrie wasn't even sure that her mother was still entitled to use it after the divorce, not that it had stopped her.

Carrie decided that since it wasn't relevant to the discussion, it was perhaps best to skip that aspect of her family history for now.

"He made his money selling a type of carriage," she told Mr Thornton.

He had actually owned a number of Jaguar, Mercedes and BMW dealerships in London and the Home Counties. Unlike her mother, who thought that money should be married, her father had had no compunction about his daughters earning their living. The brother she had mentioned was fictional.

"That's very progressive of him," Mr Thornton said.

"Yes, well things were easier in Spain."

"I thought Spain was a Roman Catholic country; very traditional in it's views."

"Well, yes, I suppose they are." How was she going to get out of this one? "But I was unmarried, you see. It's fine for a woman to work until she gets married."

"Right." He knew something was off with her stories, he just didn't know what. "Well, I'll see you tomorrow."

"Yes. And thank you again, Mr Thornton. I really appreciate this."

"My pleasure." He smiled warmly at her and her heart skipped a beat.

"Good day, Mr Thornton."

Carrie breathed a sigh of relief as she left the office. She suspected that he knew she was lying about her past, but she was keeping as close to the truth as she she could without sounding insane. She could hardly tell him that she was from the future, could she?

She gathered her wits about her once again and was about to walk out of the yard when she felt eyes on her and turned towards Mr Thornton's house. Mrs Thornton was standing at the window, staring at her. She didn't look away as Carrie spotted her and though she tried to stare the other woman down, it was Carrie who looked away first.

She suddenly didn't envy Margaret one jot, because having her as a mother-in-law really was a rather cruel and unusual punishment.

She made her way out of the yard and decided that she would visit the stationers today rather than tomorrow morning; that way she wouldn't lose any time tomorrow and could crack straight on.

Speaking of cracking straight on, she really had to try harder to cut down on her use of modern vernacular.

She arrived at the stationers and purchased some

cardboard files, some index cards and other general office supplies but the closest thing she could find to an inbox and outbox were wooden letter trays. She supposed they would suffice though and bought four of them, although they were a little expensive. Since they were also rather bulky items she asked for everything to be delivered to Marlborough Mills. Then with her receipt and very little change in hand, she headed home.

For the first time since she had arrived, she felt relaxed. Finally she had a purpose; she was doing some good by being stuck in this place and she had an income, which gave her a sense of independence.

Mr Hale was in the middle of a lesson when she got home but she brought him some tea as soon as his pupil left.

"Ah, how lovely," he said as she set the tea tray down on his desk. "How was your walk this morning?"

"Actually I wanted to talk to you about that."

"Of course, my dear, you can tell me anything."

She poured their tea and once they were settled in the chairs by the fire in his study, she began.

"Mr Hale, I didn't go for a walk this morning. I went to see about a job."

"You're leaving us?" he sounded surprised.

"Actually no. Well, that is if you don't mind me staying here."

"You are a most congenial addition to our little family, Carrie. You will always be welcome here."

"Thank you." She blushed. "Anyway, the job isn't a governess position or anything like that. I am helping out at Marlborough Mills, in the office with administration," she hastened to add. "And just for five hours a day."

"Well, that is unusual work but I suppose if it

gives you pleasure."

"It does. It also means that I have an income now and I would like to give you a portion of it."

"You don't need to pay for your room, Carrie. Besides, you don't even have your own room, you share with Margaret."

"True but if I am a member of this family then my income should benefit this family, no?"

"Well..."

"Please, Mr Hale. You and your family have been so kind taking me in and looking after me, but I know you cannot really afford one more mouth to feed. Let me help. My wage can not only save you the allowance you give me, it could pay for another servant to help Dixon. I know you don't like Margaret and I helping her as much as we do, so use this money and employ help for her."

"Well, when you put it like that, how can I refuse?"

"You can't," she said, smiling.

Chapter Five

Mr Thornton was in a foul mood the next morning, for just the afternoon before a pile of useless stationary had been delivered, costing almost all the money he had given Miss Preston. He knew he shouldn't have given her so much but he wanted to appear generous. It irked him that she seemed to think that since he gave her that money, she had carte blanche to spend it all. What did he need with four letter trays, he asked himself. It was just frivolous.

He supposed he shouldn't be surprised, most young girls were frivolous (his sister was a perfect example) but he had expected more from Miss Preston.

He ate breakfast with his mother then stood in the courtyard as the employees filed in. The bell rang for the start of work but Miss Preston was nowhere to be seen. He waited until a quarter past the hour, growing more impatient by the second. Did she think that she didn't have to keep to her times like the other mill hands?

Still, he was losing precious time himself by waiting for her so he made his way into his office. He stopped short when he found her standing by his desk, rearranging it.

"You're here!"

"Yes," she smiled. "I got here early, I wanted to press on."

He saw the letter trays laid out on his desk, three on the left hand side, one on the right. His irritation began to rise again.

"I see you had a good time at the stationers yesterday."

"What? Oh, yes. If you'll come over here I'll explain the new system to you."

"New system?" he was growing more irritable. Now she thought that she could just waltz into his office and change things as she saw fit!

"Yes. Here you have three inboxes. One for unpaid bills, one for outstanding invoices and one for other general enquiries that need your attention, such as potential bids. Once you have paid a bill, received payment or dealt with an enquiry, you put the paperwork or letters in this outbox over here so that I can file the papers away and post the letters."

She smiled at him, pleased with herself. When he didn't answer, she moved over to the filing cabinets.

"And over here, I have divided the cabinets up into suppliers, buyers and factory related - which has things like the employee tax records, inventory, cotton orders, machine parts, etcetera. The paperwork in each group is filed alphabetically, by company name for the buyers and suppliers and by subject for the factory category."

Each drawer had been labelled with it's category and which letters of the alphabet it contained.

He was ashamed to admit that her system did seem a lot more organised than his had been . It would only take him a fraction of the time to find what he needed now and he felt bad for thinking ill of her.

"You don't like it?" she said, noticing his frown.

"No. No I didn't say that," he smiled. "I am just surprised, that's all. You seem to have made things very efficient."

"Thank you. Oh, and before I forget," she went to her small purse on the table and retrieved his change and receipts which she placed on his desk.

He looked at her; she was flushed with happiness,

evidently proud of her work. He thought that he had rarely seen a more attractive sight.

"I haven't finished the filing yet, as you can see," she pointed to the stacks of papers still on the table. "But in theory at least, I think this works well."

"Indeed."

His voice was so warm that she turned to look at him and suddenly felt rather faint at the admiration she saw in his eyes. She seemed to be frozen, unable to look away or even breathe for a moment.

Mr Thornton stepped closer and Carrie wondered if he was going to kiss her. She desperately wanted him too but she also knew that he shouldn't. He wasn't hers to kiss, he belonged to Margaret.

She didn't know if she had the willpower to refuse him though and she breathed a sigh of relief when a knock sounded at his door, snapping them both out of what ever stupor had overcome them.

Carrie went back to her desk to work while John strode over to the door and opened it. His manner with Williams was somewhat curt but Carrie felt relieved. As they left she took a few moments to compose herself then set about continuing her work.

When Mr Thornton returned they worked mostly in silence until it was time for Carrie to leave, a pattern which repeated itself over the next few days.

When Sunday finally came around, Carrie had never felt so relieved to have a day off. She loved the thrill of getting up, knowing she would be seeing Mr Thornton soon but at the same time she hated working with him all morning, constantly chiding herself not to look at him lest her will fail her once again.

Sunday was a quiet day, thankfully. After attending church with the Hales, Carrie took herself off for a walk. Milton was a dirty, smoky town but up on the hills there was a modicum of fresher air and from a distance, the dirt and smoke gave the town character and made it look appealing, rather than suffocating.

Margaret may have been used to pea soupers in London but Carrie had never experienced such pollution before.

She settled herself down on the hillside and just sat there for a while, thinking.

She had been stuck in this life for a few months now and seemed no closer to getting home. It had taken her a while to get used to the manners and social mores here but she thought that she was settling in well, until Mr Bloody Thornton had to come along and make her fall in love with him!

And this was more than just being in love with his character, because that character was fictional. This Mr Thornton was just as adorable as the fictional one, only he was real, or at least he felt very real. But he wasn't meant for her, he was meant for Margaret. Margaret who looked down her nose at him. Margaret who insulted him at every turn, both intentionally and unintentionally. Margaret who didn't deserve him, damn it! It wasn't fair!

"I must be going crazy," she said softly. She was probably right at this moment lying in some insane asylum, dressed in a straightjacket and drugged out of her mind.

"I wouldn't say that."

She turned to see Mr Thornton standing behind her.

"Is this grass reserved for someone?" he asked, gesturing to the space beside her.

"Oh, no. I, uh, I like it up here, it sort of puts things in perspective, if you know what I mean."

"That's why I like walking this path too," he said,

settling beside her.

"I'm surprised," she said. "You don't really seem like the walking type."

"What type do I seem like?" he asked.

"I don't know, a bit like me I suppose, a typical city dweller, always busy, never having time to stop and smell the roses."

"And yet here we both are. I don't see any roses but there's some petunias over there that we could smell if you like."

Carrie laughed. She was seeing an aspect of to Mr Thornton's character that wasn't in the book, namely his playful side. He also had a sense of humour which Carrie had never noticed in the book. She found that she liked it very much.

"Actually I like it up here because it's quiet," Carrie admitted. "Truth be told, I'm a bit of an antisocial git. I like getting away from people and just being who I want to be for a while."

"And who do you want to be?" he asked.

Carrie turned to look at him, wondering how much she should tell this man.

"I'm not sure," she said. "But I know it's not who I'm expected to be."

"And who is that?"

Carrie sighed deeply.

"Well, my mother thinks, or rather she thought, that a woman's only role was to be pretty and marry well. My sister kind of agrees and she can't understand why I waste my time with study and work when I should be partying and meeting Mr Right. Or Mr. 'I've Got A Yacht in the South of France'. My dad, well he just bitches about women; how they're only after one thing, how they're all superficial and brainless. Of course it would help if he dated women his own age and stopped dating brain dead airheads."

"Dating?" Mr Thornton asked, for if she meant what he thought she did, then what was a married man doing courting young women?

Carrie realised her mistake, divorce was unheard of in the 1800s. Well, unless you were Henry VIII that is.

"Dating, yeah, it's um, it's just another word for flirting, really. He and my mother live, or rather lived separately and he liked to spend his free time in the company of pretty young women who flattered his ego. Nothing salacious, just a bit desperate and sad, really."

"So who do you want to be?" he asked.

"Like I said, I don't know. I know I don't want to be defined by who I marry, forever more known as 'Mr So And So's Wife'. I want to do something important, you know? Make my own mark on the world in some small way."

"You want to be famous?" he asked, unsure of her meaning.

"God no!" She cringed as she remembered Mr Hale chastising her for taking the Lord's name in vain. "Pardon me. No, what I mean is, I want to have an impact on the world, to do something that matters, that changes lives or inspires people, even if it's only a few people."

"I think that's a very worthy goal to have," he said.

"What about you, did you always want to be a cotton manufacturer or did you have another dream when you were young?"

"Me?" he sounded surprised, as though no one had ever asked him that question before. He was silent for a few moments as he thought about it. "I remember when I was a boy, I wanted to be a doctor."

"Really?"

"Does that surprise you?"

"Well yes, but only because it's so different from what you do. Was it a real goal or was it like me wanting to be a ballet dancer when I was five and a vet when I was six, and a lion tamer when I was seven?"

"A lion tamer?" he laughed.

"It's a real career I'll have you know," she grinned. "But it was just a passing fad."

"I don't know. I don't think it was a real goal." He was silent for a long while and when he spoke again his voice was low, almost like he was confessing a dark secret. "If I'm honest, I suppose I always wanted to be a scholar."

Carrie turned to him and smiled.

"I think you'd have been good at it."

"Don't flatter me," he said gruffly.

"I'm not. I've heard some of your discussions with Mr Hale and you seem very insightful."

"For someone who's never been to university, you mean." Mr Thornton was frowning.

"No, just insightful. I'm sorry, I shouldn't have started this conversation."

"Don't be. I'm not sorry for the life I lead; circumstances often dictate what we become and I've been very successful. I have no right to complain."

Carrie smiled but it was tinged with sadness.

"An engineer," she said softly.

"Who, me?" he asked, puzzled by her statement.

"No, me. It wasn't just a passing fad either, for years I've dreamed about building something that would stand the test of time and help improve lives in some way, that's why I was so interested when you were talking about the power loom the other evening. To make something like that, something that changed a whole industry... But I let myself be talked out of it and into taking soft subjects, ladylike subjects such as English."

"I don't think anyone could ever doubt that you're a lady," he said, a warm smile on his lips. "But I can see how difficult that kind of career would be for a woman."

He was judging by Victorian standards though, he didn't see her as the coward she really was for giving into her family.

"Anyway," she said, standing up. "That's enough introspection for one day. I should be getting home."

Mr Thornton stood up as well and offered her his arm.

"Then allow me to escort you," he offered.

Carrie slipped her arm through his and they strolled back down the hill towards the town.

They kept the conversation light, on topics such as music and books and when they stopped outside the small house in Crampton, Carrie thought for a moment that he was going to kiss her but instead he stepped back and, touching the brim of his hat, bid her good day.

Carrie watched him leave, pleased to note that he turned back after a dozen or so paces. She blushed to have been caught watching him and quickly made her way inside the house.

The next day Carrie was surprised to get into the office to find that Mr Thornton had moved the table she worked at so that it was opposite his desk and they now faced each other.

"I thought it was rather rude to make you face the

wall so you have to keep your back to the room," he explained. He also wanted to be able to observe her a little better.

She had finally finished rearranging the filing system on Friday and was about to ask what he wanted her to do when she noticed a stack of post was lying on her desk along with a letter opener. She duly opened the letters and put them in the relevant inboxes, then she filed the few items that had been placed in the outbox after she had left on Saturday.

Before she had finished he called her over to his desk for a moment.

"I have to go into town for a meeting shortly," he explained. "These are two bids I've worked out," he showed her his calculations. "I dug this old tender out and I was wondering if you could copy the format and write the tenders for me?"

Margaret took the sheets of paper from him and quickly read through them to make sure she understood what she had to do.

"I don't think I'll have any problems," she said.

"Good." he smiled. "If I'm not back before you go, just leave them on my desk when you're done."

She nodded her understanding. Once he had gone she finished the filing then sat back down at her desk to write the tenders.

Thankfully in the rucksack she had brought with her to this time she had a pencil case with various pens and highlighters in it. One of those pens was a fountain pen her father had given her that she used to sign her name with. She had brought it into the office after discovering how difficult it was to write using a nib and an ink well.

She had just finished the first tender when the office door opened and Mr Hale came in.

"There she is, hard at work!" he smiled. Margaret came in behind him.

"Mr Hale, how lovely to see you," she said, though she was unsure how kindly visitors during work hours would be looked upon.

"We were just returning Mrs Thornton's visit and we thought we'd stop in and see how you were getting on."

"Oh, great, thank you."

Margaret was looking around the office as though it were a museum and noticed the fountain pen sitting on her desk.

"What an unusual writing instrument," she said. "I have never seen one quite like it before."

'You should see my biro's,' Carrie thought.

"Yes, it was a gift from my father on my fourteenth birthday."

"Is it gold?" Margaret asked, shocked that such a material would be used for a pen.

"I believe so. He had the barrel inscribed with my name so it would be a kind of keepsake."

Margaret put the pen down, wondering again what kind of family this woman came from, for they seemed to have been rich and yet Carrie herself had no money. If Margaret needed any more proof of Carrie's poverty, the fact that she was working was proof enough. Perhaps her father had speculated and lost their money, much like Mr Thornton's father had.

"Well, we won't keep you," Mr Hale said. "We just wanted to see how you were getting on and say hello."

"Of course. I hope you enjoy your visit with Mrs Thornton."

Mrs Thornton had seen the Hales enter and leave the office on their way to the house so once her guests were seated, she apologised that Mr Thornton had not been there to greet them.

"Oh, that's quite all right, we really wanted to see Miss Preston," Mr Hale assured her.

"You are acquainted with my son's new assistant, then?" she asked, for she knew hardly anything about the girl. Her son seemed very protective of her and other than commenting on how good her work was, he hadn't said anything of a personal nature about her.

"Oh yes. She is my ward," Mr Hale said.

"I had no idea." Mrs Thornton said, wondering where the girl had been when she called on the Hales. "Has she been with you for long?"

"No, not long, just a few months now."

"And, I hope you don't mind me asking, but how did she come to be in your care?"

"Well, she is an orphan. I didn't feel we could turn her out into the world on her own so we invited her to live with us. Working here was her idea; she's a very independent young woman."

"Indeed," Mrs Thornton answered, though her manner was somewhat stiff. "Though I am not sure for how much longer there will be employment here. I suppose you have heard the talk of a strike?"

Mrs Thornton went on to explain all about Milton's long history of strikes and the battle that perpetually raged between the masters and workers.

Carrie quickly finished the second tender, wrote the envelopes for both and placed everything on Mr Thornton's desk for him to look over and sign.

Having run out of tasks, she went through the post in the general inbox to see if there was anything there that she thought she could handle. There wasn't so she went through the outstanding invoices to see which were the oldest and she began writing letters to those over two months old, reminding them of the invoice and that payment was now overdue. She also wrote out a copy of the original invoice in case they tried to claim that they didn't have a record of it. Though in all honesty, they had received their cotton, it was surely their duty to pay for it and if they didn't receive a bill, then to ask for it!

Still, she was used to businesses waiting as long as possible before paying their bills and if she didn't know about the financial troubles in Mr Thornton's future that the impending strike would cause, she probably wouldn't have minded so much.

The letters she wrote were firm but polite and she was just completing her third and final reminder when Mr Thornton returned.

"You're still here?" he asked. "I can't pay you past your time, you know."

Carrie looked up and realised that it was now half past two.

"I don't expect it," she answered. "Sorry, I lost track of time. Besides, Mr Hale popped in earlier on his way to see your mother, so I had some time to make up." She went back to the letter she was writing and tried not to notice how haggard Mr Thornton looked.

Mr Thornton hardly registered her words since his mind was on other things.

"Are you all right?" she finally asked, her compassion overcoming her desire to keep things professional between them.

"Aye, it's just this talk of a strike, that's all."

Carrie nodded her understanding.

"I'm sorry."

"It's hardly your fault, is it?" he asked

rhetorically.

"No, but... I just wish there was something I could do to help, that's all."

"Thank you," he smiled. "I wish there were too."

"Would you like some tea?"

"No, I'm fine. I'd best get on. You can finish whatever it is you're doing tomorrow, if you want."

"I'm nearly done."

She got back to work, pleased to note that Mr Thornton checked her tenders, signed them and slotted them into their envelopes for posting.

"Good work," he praised her. "What are you working on now?"

"Unpaid invoices," she said, handing him a copy of one of the letters she had written. "I thought a friendly reminder might be in order for those over two months old. I mean you might want me to chase up the more recent ones as well, I just thought that these were the most urgent. You may already have chased them of course, but I needed something to do."

"I haven't got around to chasing them yet," he said, reading through her letter and the attached copy invoice. "This is very good; authoritative without being rude. Good work."

"Thank you." She handed him the second letter she had finished and a few minutes later, she handed him the final letter and stood up.

"Well, if there's nothing else you need, I'll get off home now."

"Of course." Mr Thornton smiled at her. "Thank you for this," he said, holding up the letters. "I'm not sure when I would have found the time."

"You're welcome. I'll see you tomorrow," she said as she left, though in the event she saw him again that evening.

Chapter Six

Mr Thornton called at the house in Crampton later that day to apologise for not keeping his lesson with Mr Hale the night before and at the same time, he discreetly gave Margaret the contact details for Dr Donaldson. Carrie surmised that Margaret must have asked for the details when she visited Mrs Thornton today and looked over at Mrs Hale, who was indeed looking rather pale and listless these days.

Mr Thornton stayed for tea and before long the conversation turned to the strike. Margaret got into quite a heated discussion with Mr Thornton over his handling of his financial affairs. She wanted him to be more open with his workers but Carrie could understand his reticence. In her time, most people were more likely to talk about their sex lives than their financial affairs.

Of course in this case, Margaret was right and his only hope of stopping a strike was to be open and honest with his workforce.

This discussion led on to his right to influence his workers lives, with Margaret feeling that it was his Christian duty as someone with power over them to tell them what to do away from work, and he arguing that his workers deserved their independence when they were on their own time.

"You must have seen for yourself by now, how independent we Darkshire men are, Miss Hale. What right do I have to dictate how my workers live their lives merely because they have labour to sell and I have the capital to buy it?"

"No, not because of your labour and capital, but because you are a man dealing with a group of men over whom you have immense power and simply because your life and theirs are so interwoven."

This was something that had always troubled Carrie in the book and so she spoke up now.

"Margaret, God gave man free will so that he might make his own choices. I don't understand why you believe that Mr Thornton has the right to take that god-given free will away from them? Not to mention what would happen if the master should not be quite so upstanding? What if he led his workers into sin? We have free will so that we can make our own decisions and the most other people can do is to try and educate us about which choices are better than others."

"That is hardly the point."

"Then what is the point?" Carrie asked. "If I were to employ your father, should I have the right to dictate how he and you live your lives?"

"Well, no..."

"Why not?"

"Well, because you are a woman."

"Indeed I am, but I dare say I am more knowledgeable about many things than most men."

Margaret laughed and Carrie bristled.

"I know that you lack even the most basic understanding of how the human mind works! You haven't got a clue how or why people think the way they do or how their behaviour can be influenced. Group dynamics are playing a massive role in this confrontation because the workers identify with each other more than they do with the masters and to convince them that they and their kind are wrong and that the masters are right is an uphill struggle. In this conversation, Margaret, you are like a child trying to tell the grown ups how to behave."

Margaret was looking rather affronted and Carrie

suddenly felt bad.

"I'm sorry, I shouldn't have spoken to you like that, but I am getting sick and tired of being told that I am inferior just because by an accident of birth, I am female."

"It was not an accident," Margaret said. "It was God's choice."

"Very well." Though she was still affronted by Margaret's sexism, it had sidetracked her. "Mr Thornton here employs your father to teach him the classics. As such, do you believe he has just as much right to dictate how your father lives as he does his workers?"

"Well no, of course not," Margaret was clearly out of her depth and floundering for an answer. But then poor Margaret hadn't had the luxury of being schooled in the art of arguing by the St Catherine's School for Girls debate club, as Carrie had.

"Why?"

"Well, because... I suppose because, and I know you will not like this, Papa, but it is true. Mr Thornton is not a gentleman."

'Classist and sexist,' Carrie thought, wondering somewhat meanly if she could goad Margaret into the trifecta of expressing racist views as well.

To her surprise, Mr Thornton didn't seem to take any offence at Margaret's remark; rather he seemed to be enjoying their debate.

"You would have been better off arguing that Mr Thornton and I had no right to dictate to your father because he is a man of the church, rather than branding us both as inferior to him. I realise that you are a product of your time, Margaret, and I really shouldn't berate you for that fact, but there are as many gentleman and members of the nobility out there who are a total waste of space as there are good, decent, hard working, poor people. I should much rather trust the judgement of someone who works for a living over that of the idle rich, who wile away their days in lives of care and ease. How can they possibly understand what life is like for a working man, let alone a poor man?"

Everyone seemed to have been rendered speechless by her diatribe and, realising that she was tackling topics that these people were far from wanting to hear about, Carrie decided it was best if she excused herself and went into Mr Hale's study downstairs. Truth be told, she felt rather foolish for even daring to voice such opinions in this time. Deep down she knew that her views were right but still, something about living in this day and age made her feel that she was the one in the wrong.

She heard the conversation continue between Mr Hale and Mr Thornton but she couldn't make out their words. She picked up Plato's Republic, which had been mentioned earlier in the conversation, and sat down to read it. She had no idea how long she had been sitting there when he came in.

"Miss Preston?" She looked up to see Mr Thornton peering around the door. "I'm not disturbing you, I hope."

"Oh, no. I am sorry about my outburst up there but sometimes I get tired of everyone having opinions they are certain are true but can't back up with facts. My father always said that unless you can argue your opinion on a given subject, you don't have a right to hold an opinion but so many people here argue with half truths and anecdotes. What about facts, reason and logic?"

"Do you believe me guilty of the same crime?" he asked.

"In some areas, yes, but your opinion on the mills

must be respected because of your experience, even if some of your ideas about your employees need a little updating."

"Updating?" he asked.

"I only mean that, although the masters are locked in a struggle with their men, it would be better for everyone involved if you could find a way to understand each other and come to a compromise."

"You are right, of course, but I doubt that will happen in my lifetime."

"Someone once told me that you have to be the change you want to see."

Mr Thornton smiled at such idealistic words, thinking them naive.

"Plato?" he asked, noticing the cover of the book she held.

"I thought I'd give it a try, I haven't read it before."

"And what do you think so far?"

"Well, so far the descriptions of the Utopia seem rather outdated and bear very little resemblance to most modern societies. In fact if I'm being honest, it sounds more like a dictatorship than Utopia."

Mr Thornton smiled, impressed with her answer, for it was a rare man who could so readily form an opinion, let alone a woman.

"Are you sure you have never read that book before?" he asked.

"No, I prefer fiction usually."

"And you have never heard it spoken of before."

Carrie's smile faltered.

"Are you asking me whether I've formed this opinion myself or if I have simply stolen someone else's idea?" Her voice held a note of warning.

"I suppose I am." He had the good grace to

look sheepish.

"Then I'm afraid I can't dignify your question with an answer. Good evening, Mr Thornton."

Seeing that he was being well and truly dismissed for underestimating her, he left.

Her earlier words had sounded idealistic and impractical but he couldn't get that phrase out of his head; *'be the change you want to see'*. He wanted change, that was certain but how could he, only one man, affect such change?

Chapter Seven

Carrie returned home from work to find that Mr Hale was out but Dr Donaldson had just been to see Mrs Hale and the news wasn't good. She comforted Margaret as best she could and was grateful that the girl never seemed to hold a grudge against her when Carrie went off on one at her. She was a much more forgiving person than Carrie had ever given her credit for when she read the book.

Margaret wanted to be alone to see her mother and, being wise enough to realise that this was a family time, Carrie took herself off for another long walk.

The doctor had diagnosed consumption, which Carrie knew was what tuberculosis was often called. Unfortunately she also knew that while easily treated with antibiotics in her time, here there was no treatment. She knew that antibiotics came from mould but she had no idea how to extract penicillin from mould.

'The Internet would know,' she thought sadly.

Though this wasn't the first time since arriving here that she missed the Internet, she didn't think she had ever felt the loss of that resource quite as greatly as she did right now.

She stopped in at the apothecary and picked up more willow bark as well as some laudanum, which she knew was basically morphine. It would ease Mrs Hale's pain as the disease progresses and help suppress her cough reflex, which would surely only be a relief once the disease began to ravage her lungs.

With little else to do, she began walking around the town, just wandering really, trying to get to know the place a little better.

Finally, realising that it was getting quite late, she turned to head in the direction she thought their house in Crampton was. She didn't notice Mr Thornton behind her, or hear his calls since one of the mills or factories around here had just let out and the streets were suddenly thronged with people. She began to feel herself being buffeted about by them. Some who passed her began cat-calling and pretty soon hands began to touch and grab at her.

Carrie slapped the hands away as best she could but before she knew it, she was pushed face first into a wall and pressed against it by someone behind her. Instinct and her self-defence training kicked in and with a roar, the heel of her boot came squarely down on his foot and less than a second later, her elbow went into his ribs. As soon as she was free she spun around and although her attacker was on the ground clutching his foot, it appeared he wasn't alone and his friends did not take kindly to their mate being beaten up by a girl.

The first friend came at her, intending to grab her shoulders but a swift kick to the groin put him out of action. The second friend was clever enough to realise that she was a fighter and decided to be more forceful and subdue her with a punch. She hadn't turned to him quickly enough to block the first blow and it landed squarely on her cheek bone. The second blow she managed to block with her arm, then she kicked out, hitting him squarely in the shin and as his head instinctively lowered, the heel of her left hand connected with his nose, breaking it. He reeled away, clutching his nose but the first attacker was now on his feet again, though still limping quite badly.

'Good,' Carrie thought with satisfaction. 'I hope

his foot's broken!'

Unfortunately, though wounded, his injury did seem to have made him rather angry. A crowd had formed around them to watch and Carrie wondered why they were just standing there. Perhaps this passed as sport up here, or perhaps they were enjoying her winning the fight. Either way, she thought that a little help would have been nice right about now.

Her attacker took in the state of his friends and, fuelled by hurt pride, he ran at her. He was out of control, she realised and rather than fight him, she quickly dodged out of the way at the last moment and he hit the wall, although he managed to break the impact with his hands and quickly turned on her again.

Carrie picked her skirts up with her hands and as he ran at her once more, with a roar of aggression she kicked high into the air, hitting him squarely in the solar plexus. Unfortunately her skirts, petticoats and boots weren't made for fighting so she tripped and landed on her hip, though she quickly climbed back to her feet as best she could, just in time to hear someone yelling for everyone to clear out.

Never had she been so pleased to hear someone's voice and as the workers began to disperse, she ran at Mr Thornton, wrapping her arms around his neck.

He quickly took in the scene before him and while he silently praised her bravery at taking these three men on, he cursed himself for having been so slow to reach her. He held her tightly, keeping an eye on her attackers.

Seconds later he heard the sound of whistles and the last of the bystanders moved away as the police arrived.

Somewhat reluctantly, Carrie detached herself

from Mr Thornton, apologising to him for her forward behaviour.

The police arrested the men, though they clearly didn't believe her when she said that she had felled them. Mr Thornton backed her account up though, since he had seen what happened as he ran down the hill towards her.

"You'd best be careful when the whistle sounds in future, Miss," one of the officers told her.

"I didn't realise it was so late," she said, for the evenings were growing much lighter.

"Are you done?" Mr Thornton asked the policemen.

"Aye."

"I'll see Miss Preston home then," he said, guiding her away from the scene. "Are you sure you are all right?" he asked when they were out of earshot of the policemen.

"I'll be fine," she assured him, though she could already feel her control slipping.

He took her to the mill as it was closer than her home and led her into his house. His mother and sister stood up in shock as they came in to the parlour and Carrie figured that she must look a bit of a sight.

"Well, not exactly the first impression I wanted to make," she joked but as she went to laugh, a sob escaped her instead and she began to cry.

Mr Thornton gathered her into his arms and held her while she cried, stroking her back and cooing softly to her.

She pulled away as soon as she had herself reasonably under control again.

"I'm sorry, I think the shock just caught up with me."

"Nonsense," he reassured her. "Now, sit down

and let's get you cleaned up."

Whilst she had been crying, evidently his mother had gone for supplies as she shooed her son out of the way, sat Carrie down and began to clean her cheek with a cloth and a bowl of warm water.

"The skin doesn't look broken," Mrs Thornton said. "But you'll have a nasty bruise come morning."

"What happened?" Fanny asked.

"She was attacked," Mr Thornton explained. "Three men from Hampers tried to get a little fresh with her, but she put them in their place."

Mrs Thornton began to clean Carrie's hands, evidently expecting to find abrasions under the blood but there was nothing.

"It's not my blood," she explained. "I broke one of their noses."

"Where did you learn to do that?" John asked.

"I studied karate for a while."

"Karate?"

"It's a martial art from the Far East. It's a combination of fighting skill, discipline and philosophy."

"And why did you yell when you struck them?" he asked, for he had never seen anything like her display before.

"It helps to channel aggression and to unnerve your opponent."

"You learned to fight?" Fanny said, quite disgusted by the idea.

"No, the point of martial arts isn't to become a good fighter but rather to end violence swiftly when it occurs. I have never attacked anyone in my life; only defended myself."

"Well I think it very unseemly."

Carrie thought it best not to answer since Fanny's

mind was obviously made up and she didn't want an argument.

"What do you think John?" Fanny asked, clearly not willing to let the point rest. "I'm quite sure that none of my friends would have behaved in such a manner."

"I think you're right," he agreed with her, his tone neutral.

"See!" Fanny smiled as though she had won the argument. It was this smugness that finally goaded Carrie into defending her actions.

"Then perhaps I should have just let them do with me as they wanted until some big, strong man found the time to ride to my rescue, but who knows what greater evils might have been done to me in that time than damaging my reputation through fighting."

Her sarcasm wasn't lost of Fanny, who harrumphed with displeasure.

"Well, what were you doing out alone? I never go anywhere without mother or a servant."

"Then what a very small and dull life you must lead, Miss Thornton. I don't like to rely on others or become a burden to them. I much prefer being able to take care of myself. Besides, I've been hurt worse than this horse riding, and I do that for fun."

"You horse ride?" Fanny asked, suddenly sounding much more friendly.

"Yes. I used to have my own horses."

"Really? What were they like?"

Carrie didn't really think that Fanny would become a friend but in the interests of civility she answered the question.

"My first mount was a black pony called Friday. She was gorgeous. I learned to ride on her and I kept her even after I was too big to ride her. She became a companion to my next horse, Milly, a chestnut thoroughbred. She could be a little temperamental at times but she was a lovely horse."

"What happened to them?"

"Friday slipped on the hard ground in the field one winter; she broke her leg and had to be put to sleep. When I went-" she remembered that women didn't go to university here. "When I returned from Spain, I left Milly with a friend of mine."

"Oh, I adore horses, I would love to learn to ride."

"Well, if you want to get serious about it, it's pretty dangerous. I can't tell you how many times I've fallen off. I've broken my wrist, my finger and two toes, I dislocated my shoulder once and have suffered so many cuts and bruises that I couldn't even begin to count them."

"You're rather accident prone then?" Mr Thornton said with an amused smile.

"Hardly. I used to love show jumping, cross country and puissance, all rather high risk activities, I'm afraid."

"Did you hunt?" Fanny asked.

"No, I think it's cruel and barbaric. I can't stand it."

Once again Fanny looked taken aback.

"What's puissance?" John asked, hoping to divert the conversation on to safer ground.

"There's only one jump and it gets higher and higher each round until only one horse and rider remains. If you knock the jump over, then you're out. The highest I ever managed to jump was just under six feet on Milly. That was taller than she was at the withers."

John looked at this woman before him with a new found respect. She had talked about not being inferior to men but now he could see that it was more than just talk. She had bravery which was uncommon among her sex and took a control over her own life and destiny that few ladies did.

"There," Mrs Thornton said when she had finished cleaning Carrie's hands. "There's not too much damage."

"Do you have a mirror?" Carrie asked.

Mrs Thornton gestured to the mirror over the fireplace and Carrie went to look at her cheek.

"I should be able to cover that with makeup," she said.

"You mean paint?" Fanny gasped, clearly affronted once again.

Carrie took a deep breath so that she didn't shout.

"I really am getting quite tired of being judged by you, Miss Thornton. Yes, I mean paint or whatever you want to call it, something to disguise the bruising and if you really think a little bit of makeup is so scandalous, then perhaps you should ask yourself why?"

"No decent woman wears paint."

"I can assure you my dear, I am every inch the decent woman and my pedigree is far superior to yours." Carrie turned to her. "The problem with social climbers is that they feel the need to judge everyone else. You belittle others because you don't feel as if you belong to the class you wish to. It's a telltale sign of a social climber. If you want to fit in and appear middle or upper class, I suggest that you learn to be a little more tolerant and treat the lowest of the working classes with exactly the same courtesy as you would show Queen Victoria, should you ever be lucky enough meet her."

"If you're so superior, then why are you working in John's factory?"

"I said my pedigree was superior, I didn't say I was. I prefer to pay my own way rather than being a burden to others and I see nothing shameful in working; in fact I quite enjoy it. The class I was born into is simply a matter of chance and has very little to do with the kind of person I am or wish to be. I prefer to judge people on their character, not their class."

Knowing that she couldn't argue that trade was shameful without offending her mother and brother, Fanny returned to the earlier point.

"And what does it say about your character that you wear paint?"

"You know nothing of my character but you assume based on one comment that I am some harlot." Well, in truth by Victorian standards she was, but she had no intention of letting Fanny win this argument. "I rather think that wanting to cover up a bruise and not become the subject of attention and gossip shows a sense of decorum, though now that I have met you, I can see that there is no way I can avoid becoming the talk of Milton." She took a deep breath. "Now, I really think that I have made quite enough of a show of myself for one evening and I had better return home before the Hales begin to worry. They have enough on their plate at the moment."

"Nothing serious, I hope?" Mr Thornton asked.

Carrie's gaze shot to Fanny. She didn't so much mind being the subject of local gossip herself but she didn't want Mrs Hale to be subjected to it.

"Let me see you home," Mr Thornton offered.

"I'm fine, honestly. Thank you for your help earlier, I don't know what I'd have done if you hadn't come along when you did."

"Nonsense, you wiped the floor with them."

Carrie smiled but she was beginning to feel rather tired now that the adrenalin was wearing off.

"Let me see you home," he asked again. "Please."

Carrie nodded, accepting his offer. She felt better when she was with him and right now, even if it was inconveniencing him, she wanted to feel good.

"Well," Fanny huffed once they had left. "I have never been so insulted in all my life!"

Mrs Thornton actually admired the girl in many ways, for she could see her own indomitable spirit in her. Unfortunately she also saw how her son looked at her and couldn't help but think that the girl was so wild that she would surely make him the talk of Milton, and not in a good way.

No, this association was not to be encouraged in the slightest and until the day John came to her, telling her of his intentions towards Miss Preston, she would not accept the possibility.

"Are you really okay?" John asked as they sat in the cab. "You're wincing."

"I think my hip is bruised," she confessed. "But I got some willow bark for Mrs Hale today; I can take some of that to help with the pain if necessary."

"Is Mrs Hale worse?" he asked.

"I'm afraid so. Mr Hale is still mostly ignorant, I think he wants to believe she can recover, but Dr Donaldson visited today and I think it is a lost cause."

"I'm sorry to hear that," he said, taking her hand to comfort her.

"Thank you," she said, squeezing his hand.

"What for?"

"For being so understanding, for coming along when you did. For not calling me a brazen hussy for daring to defend myself and talking about makeup."

"You could never be a hussy in my eyes."

Tears pricked at her eyes and she smiled, for she really had experienced more than her fair share of being judged and found wanting since she had arrived in this place.

"Besides, I know you'd beat me up if I did," he teased.

Carrie laughed and Mr Thornton found himself captivated by her smile. On impulse he reached out with his free hand and gently caressed her bruised cheek. Her laughter faded rather abruptly as the mood in the cab changed. He leaned in closer and gently kissed her, his lips barely brushing hers. When she didn't pull away, he deepened the kiss.

For a moment, Carrie gave herself up to her desire, relishing the feel of his lips on hers, the gentle caress of his finger as he stroked her cheek with the back of his hand, the strong, masculine scent of him that threatened to overwhelm her and make her swoon as Victorian ladies were prone to do in novels.

All too soon however, the carriage slowed to a stop and Mr Thornton pulled away. Carrie suddenly remembered that he wasn't hers, he was Margaret's and here she was, about to destroy the greatest romance that she had ever known!

Embarrassed and ashamed, she ran from the cab and into the house, pausing to lean against the door after she closed it while she caught her breath. She half expected Mr Thornton to knock but he didn't and after a few moments she headed up to her room.

"Carrie, is that you my dear?"

"Yes, Mr Hale. I'll be back in a moment but the streets are rather dusty today and I need to wash."

She bolted up to her room and closed the door behind her. She pulled her mirror out of her handbag and surveyed the damage to her face. The bruise was already showing quite a bit but she thought that she could cover it well, especially since it was finally growing dark outside and the only light would be from candles. She hurriedly changed into clean clothes, pausing only briefly to survey the bruise that was forming on her hip, then she found a packet of matches to light her own candle. Sitting close by it, she used her concealer to cover the bruise and then dabbed some powder over the top to set it.

Considering the poor light, it probably wasn't the best job she had ever done but it seemed to look okay. And the light would be no better downstairs.

Thankfully her concealer was fairly new, as was her compact so she should have more than enough to keep her bruise covered for the next week or so until it faded.

She headed down stairs to sit with the family.

"We were getting worried about you," Mr Hale said, smiling as she came in. "You missed dinner."

"Yes, I'm sorry. I lost track of time and then I just got lost and it took me a while to find a cab to bring me home."

"Well, I'm sure Dixon has saved you something." He got up to ring the bell.

"No, don't. I'll go down and see her."

Dixon had kept some stew which she warmed up for her. Carrie ate in the kitchen, then returned to the family and sat reading until her eyes grew heavy and she excused herself to bed.

"I do not think that working agrees with her," Mrs Hale said after she had left. "It is very early for one so young to be tired."

"Perhaps she has just walked further than normal today," Margaret said. "She has not looked tired on other nights."

"No indeed, she is quite a formidable young woman," Mr Hale added.

Carrie listened from the stairwell as hot tears streamed over her face. She certainly didn't feel very formidable right now.

Carrie stayed in bed until Margaret had risen the next day so that she could apply her makeup in peace. If 'paint' was indeed looked down upon, she didn't want the Hales to know she was wearing any, nor indeed why she was wearing it.

There was a good light as she sat in front of the window and although it took two layers of concealer, she thought that she did a pretty good job covering the bruise. After she applied the face powder over the top, she also added a tiny bit of blusher, just to trick the eye to notice the colour rather than the slight swelling of her cheek.

Because she had stayed in bed she had to rush through breakfast so that she could make it to work on time, but given how little she was looking forward to seeing Mr Thornton today, she didn't mind not having time to think.

He wasn't in the office when she arrived so she sat down and began opening and sorting his post. He came in about an hour later and she turned and smiled warmly at him.

"Morning, boss," she said, her tone bright but brittle.

"Miss Preston. How are you today?"

"Well aside from being a fallen, painted lady, I'm fine."

He walked up to her and she turned her cheek to him so that he could see for himself.

"I'd never know if I didn't know what to

look for."

"Good." She nodded.

There was an uncomfortable silence for a moment until Mr Thornton finally broached the subject that they had been avoiding.

"Miss Preston, I want to apologise for my behaviour yesterday. I should never have been so forward with you. My actions were unforgivable and I apologise."

Carrie put the letter she was holding down and turned to him.

"I'm not offended," she said. "I... I like you, a lot. An awful lot. More than I should because... well you weren't meant for me and the fact that we have feelings for each other is just... well it's weird, if you must know. Please don't think you offended my morality or anything, because I enjoyed it. It's just..."

"I'm meant for someone else?" he finished uncertainly.

"Exactly."

"Did you have anyone specific in mind?"

"Yes. And no. It's complicated."

"So you are refusing me because you believe me to be in love with another."

"Exactly." In the book he was already madly in love with Margaret. He may like Carrie, but he surely must also have feelings for Margaret.

"I hate to break it to you, Miss Preston, but no one else outside of my family has any kind of hold over my heart."

Carrie looked down. Oh no, what had she done!

"You look upset," he noted.

"I am."

"Why?"

"Because... Oh, because it's all wrong, that's why.

Nothing is going the way it should and that's my fault." She felt tears sting her eyes but did her best to blink them back.

"How is it your fault?"

"Because I'm not supposed to be here," she confessed. "I'm supposed to be studying in London with my family."

Mr Thornton knelt down in front of her.

"I know tragedies can happen but you must not blame yourself. Wherever your family are now, do you not think that they would want you to be happy?"

He was being so kind to her, but it was all a lie because her family wasn't dead! That only served to make her feel worse; she didn't deserve his sympathy. Finally Carrie could hold her tears back no longer and they spilled out over her cheeks.

"Hey." He reached out and gently wiped a tear away with his thumb. "Don't cry. I'm sorry I upset you."

"I don't deserve you, Mr Thornton. The affection you feel for me shouldn't be mine. I've ruined everything."

Though he didn't know what she meant, he could see that her pain was genuine.

"Do you suppose that one day you might explain these odd statements?" he asked kindly. "For whilst they sound like nonsense, I think they are a very large part of understanding who you are."

Carrie looked into his eyes.

"If I told you the truth, you would think I was crazy."

"Do you really believe so little of me?"

"No," she managed a wry smile. "But half the time, I think I'm crazy."

"We will talk no more of this now," he said,

gently wiping her cheeks with his handkerchief. "I have upset you and you don't trust me. I hope that at some point you will open up to me and come to realise that how I feel about you is very real and very right."

Carrie nodded and turned back to her work as Mr Thornton stood up and sat back down at his desk. They both got on with their work, doing their best to ignore the undercurrent of tension that existed between them; a pattern that repeated itself for the rest of the week. Then, as if her misery was not enough already, on the Friday the workers went on strike.

With no work to do at the mill, Carrie stayed home most days, helping Dixon. Mr Thornton had said that she could continue to come in and that he would find work for her, but she didn't want him to be paying her for jobs that didn't really need doing, so she declined his offer.

She also did her best to avoid him when he came to his lessons with Mr Hale. He needed a chance to get to know Margaret and so she made herself scarce every time he arrived.

After two weeks there was no sign of the strike ending and so Carrie tried to find work elsewhere. Not only was she feeling the loss of her wages, she knew that Mr Hale had lost some of his students, or they had at least cut back on their lessons and money was tighter than ever.

Carrie asked for work in shops mainly but was consistently refused. It seemed that Mr Hale and the mill masters weren't the only ones feeling the financial pinch from the strike.

Word got back to Mr Thornton that a young lady was seeking employment and he guessed who it was. It hurt him that she had refused his offer of work during the strike but was happy to seek employment elsewhere, though he supposed after the shocking way he had behaved toward her when he kissed her, he could not blame her for not wanting to see him.

Besides, despite her fine words about judging people based on their character, he wasn't sure that extended to actually marrying a manufacturer. Though it pained him to admit it, she was far too good for the likes of him.

During the third week of the strike he set about importing hands from Ireland while his mother prepared for her annual dinner party. He was disquieted to hear that Mr Hale had only replied for three. It could be that Mrs Hale was too unwell to attend, or it could be that Miss Preston was still avoiding him, for he was astute enough to realise that was what she was doing.

Fanny was quite put out about the fact that Miss Preston had been invited, while his mother declared her to be wild and hoped that she did not upset her other guests with her antics.

Mr Thornton rather hoped she would, for he was almost certain that she could argue her point with almost anyone and he enjoyed watching her. He did not know that she had been captain of a debateing team in school, nor that her knowledge gained at GCSE far surpassed that of most educated people in the 1850s, simply because more had been discovered and was understood by the 21st century.

When the evening of the dinner party arrived, Miss Preston looked every inch the lady, putting everyone else there in her shadow without seeming to try, at least to Mr Thornton's eye.

Though she had bought a few dresses of her own now, Carrie didn't have anything suitable for a dinner party and once again Margaret had ridden to her rescue, offering her a choice of her silk gowns from London.

Carrie chose a dusky pink dress with a low, off the shoulder neckline, a fitted bodice and a flared skirt. The neckline had been adorned with roses, as had the seams of the bodice but Carrie wasn't really a flowery kind of person (she wasn't a pink kind of person either, but this shade wasn't too bad). She removed the roses by hand and replaced them with piping in a slightly darker shade of pink that drew attention to the lines of the bodice and made the dress look altogether more streamlined and less flouncy.

It had taken her hours to make the piping and then sew it on but the effect was worth it; plus it helped to keep her busy now that she was unemployed. She kept a few of the roses from the dress, unpicked them and made larger roses from them, adding some pink lace and some pink feathers which she bought from the haberdashery, to fashion a hair ornament that would match the dress.

The skirts on her day dresses weren't too outlandish but the much wider, bell shaped skirts on the evening dresses took some getting used to. Though thankfully, since they were in reduced circumstances, the Hales still had to make do with petticoats under their skirts rather than the crinoline cages which were becoming fashionable. Carrie had yet to experience a crinoline cage personally but from Dixon's description she thought they sounded rather stupid, but then she was a girl who preferred worn jeans and baggy jumpers.

Corsets were also something Carrie was having trouble getting used to. An ill fitting corset could chafe, restrict breathing and be downright painful so

Dixon had insisted that she have her own made at the earliest opportunity and that it was of the best quality. Thankfully the current fashion wasn't too narrow at the waist but it was still made with whale bone which greatly restricted her movement. Bending over was impossible, which she freely admitted was good for the back, though it was also incredibly inconvenient when she dropped something on the floor.

She still had only her black boots to wear with the dress but the skirt was so long that no one would probably even see her feet.

Her bruise was well healed by now but she wore a little mascara to emphasise her eyes and a touch of lipstick to darken her lips very slightly. Makeup had always been a form of war paint to Carrie, something to hide behind when she needed to and right now she needed to hide, for the very idea of seeing Mr Thornton again terrified her; not so much how he would react to her but more how she would react to him after having successfully avoided him for so long.

She had tried to get out of going, arguing that someone should stay and keep Mrs Hale company but Mrs Hale wouldn't hear if it. It seemed she wanted to live vicariously through the others and Carrie couldn't refuse without seriously upsetting a dying woman, something that she didn't particularly want on her conscience.

As they left the house, Carrie noticed the lamp lighter climbing up a ladder with his spirit torch to light the gas street lamp outside their house. She had found it strange and worrying when she first arrived here, for the light came from a naked flame rather than using a gas mantle, which resembled a light bulb and gave a much brighter light. It still made her uneasy to see the flames but she was slowly getting used to the idea that the street lights would not explode. Still, a part of her was glad that the Hales could not afford a larger house which might well also be lit with gas. As far as Carrie was concerned, candles were enough of a risk but at least they could be easily blown out. She knew that she would probably never rest easy if the house was lit with open gas flames.

Margaret's friend, Bessy, came to see them off to the dinner party since she was anxious to see Margaret dressed up in her finery. Carrie thought that Bessy was looking very pale for one so young and although she tried to stifle it, Carrie noticed her coughing. Her heart plummet as she watched them talk briefly, for Carrie knew from the book that it would not be very much longer now until Bessy succumbed to the cotton fluff on her lungs and died.

Margaret must have also noticed that Bessy didn't look as well as usual for she was very subdued on the cab ride to the Thorntons. She had also been feeling guilty about going to this dinner party at all when so many in Milton were living on or below the breadline thanks to the strike but Bessy had been insistent that Margaret go since she wanted to see her friend dressed in her London finery.

As they alighted from the cab in the mill yard, they each took one of Mr Hale's arms and he guided them into the house. Thankfully they were greeted by Mrs Thornton as Mr Thornton didn't seem to be around. They mingled with the other guests, chatting about nothing in particular and avoiding talk of the strike at all costs. Carrie was rather practised at small talk, though she didn't much enjoy it.

Carrie hadn't met many of the people who were

here but Mr Hale had met a few of the mill owners through Mr Thornton. There were also two merchants and their wives, as well a gentleman named Mr Southard, an MP from Lampton, the next town over. Carrie listened with interest as he, Mr Hale and one of the mill owners, Mr Slickson began a discussion on the relevance of the church in modern life.

Mr Slickson could see no role for the church beyond keeping people in line with the threat of going to hell but Mr Hale and Mr Southard saw that the church could act as a check against men of power abusing those beneath them. Indeed many of the more recent laws to protect workers from inhumane working conditions were proposed by some of the more devout members of parliament, thanks to their Christian conscience. Mr Southard aptly noted that without the church and the Sabbath, the working man wouldn't even have one day of rest a week.

Though she was still listening to the exchange with interest, Carrie felt rather than saw when Mr Thornton entered the room, for she felt as if she was was suddenly surrounded by static electricity. She could almost feel his eyes warming her skin as he looked at her. Unable to stop herself, she turned to him and the passion she saw in his gaze as he drank in her image made her feel light headed.

Of course, some of that might well be thanks to the rather restrictive corset on her dress but she doubted it. No man had ever made her feel like this before; so careless and carefree! She wanted to hurl herself at him and kiss him as if her life depended on it, bystanders be damned! But she didn't. Somehow she managed to smile and remain where she was.

He approached her and they shook hands. Carrie lowered her eyes suddenly feeling self-conscious under his hungry gaze.

"I'm so glad you could come," he said, so far completely ignoring the others to whom she had been talking.

"Thank you." She smiled, wishing she could think of something more interesting to say to him.

"I was sorry to hear that Mrs Hale couldn't join us," he said, reluctantly glancing at Mr Hale, though his gaze soon returned to Carrie.

"She is sorry as well, but she has made Margaret and Carrie promise to give her a full account of events." Mr Hale smiled, oblivious to Mr Thornton's interest in his ward.

"Thornton," Slickson interrupted their moment and Mr Thornton reluctantly let go of Carrie's hand. "Good to see you again."

Carrie tried to listen to their conversation but more often than not she found herself staring at Mr Thornton, thinking a lot of rather impure thoughts about what she wished he would do to her!

Finally Mr Hamper interrupted them and called Mr Thornton away, lessening her torment for a while. Mr Southard took it upon himself to introduce her and Margaret to some of those in the room who they hadn't met before and, though she was always aware of exactly where Mr Thornton was in relation to her, Carrie never looked at him.

Finally Mrs Thornton announced that dinner was served and Mr Southard escorted Margaret into the dining room while Mr Hale escorted Carrie.

The dinner was exquisite, though given how rich the food was and how restricting her corset was, Carrie finally understood why ladies in the Victorian era seemed to nibble their food rather than eat it.

Mostly the women just listened while the men talked until finally the conversation turned to the taboo subject of the strike.

Fanny questioned Margaret about her taking food to the Princeton district and Margaret explained about John Boucher and his starving children.

"Well, he knows what to do," Hamper said. "Go back to work."

"If only it were that easy," Carrie sighed.

"I'm sorry?" Mr Thornton asked her.

Carrie blushed, for she hadn't meant to say that out loud.

"I said, if only it were as easy as just going back to work."

"Why wouldn't it be?" Hamper asked her.

"The unions have immense power over these men," she explained. "If they refuse to join the union or go against the strike, they become outcasts among their people. No one will help them, speak to them or even look at them. Imagine living your life being shunned by everyone around you? Who here would be brave enough to defy the union under threat of those penalties?"

"How do you know this?" Mr Thornton asked her.

"I read a lot and have learned something of the union practices." Well she could hardly say that she had read about it in North and South, could she?

"So you're telling me that if a man returns to work without the backing of the union, he's an outcast?" Mr Southard asked, seemingly very interested in this news even though he had nothing to do with manufacturing.

"Yes," she confirmed.

"For how long?" Mr Slickson asked.

"Until they tow the line again by doing whatever it is the union wants them to do, I suppose. There are many men who would dearly love to return to work, and many who didn't want to strike in the first instance, but they are afraid of the repercussions if they do not do as the union says."

The men looked at each other, all wondering if this was true and if so, how it would affect them.

"Mr Higgins has said something similar to me about the ways and means of the unions," Margaret confirmed. "And I know for a fact that Boucher would like to return to work."

"It looks as though both sides in this war know very little of what the other side is up to," Mr Southard observed. "The workers think you are cutting their pay to increase your profits rather than weathering hard times, while you think that each and every worker sides with the union, when it appears that many don't."

"Perhaps if you could talk with the union leaders," Margaret added, smiling at the M.P. "You might be able to come to an understanding."

"There's too much distrust," Slickson said.

"Aye, for you," Mr Thornton said pointedly.

The conversation moved on after that but as the women left to go to the drawing room, Carrie could hear the conversation turn back to the union. She wanted to stay and hear what they had to say (and maybe share their cigars and brandy!) but that would not be seemly in this day and age.

The men joined the ladies again a little later but soon afterwards the evening broke up. As their carriage pulled away from the house, Carrie couldn't help but look back at the house and was surprised to see Mr Thornton still on the front step, watching her leave.

She was not surprised to see Mrs Thornton watching from the sitting room like some Greek goddess surveying her subjects. The look she gave Carrie did not show great affection and indeed if she had possessed the power of the Greek gods, Carrie was in little doubt that after receiving such a harsh look, she would be turning to stone right about now.

A few days later Dr Donaldson suggested that they ask to borrow the Thornton's water mattress for Mrs Hale since he believed it would help her to rest more easily. Margaret offered to go and Carrie was both pleased and devastated.

She was pleased because this was a pivotal point in John and Margaret's relationship but she was devastated because selfishly, she wanted to keep Mr Thornton's affection to herself.

But she knew that this must happen, that Margaret must protect Mr Thornton and so she bit her tongue and stayed home while Margaret went to enquire about the mattress.

When Margaret returned home little more than an hour later, unharmed and without having seen Mr Thornton, Carrie grew worried.

Surely today was the day of the riot? Had her presence in this place altered events to such a degree that there would be no riot?

Somehow Carrie couldn't believe that.

"What was the town like?" Carrie asked.

"Very quiet, actually. I'm not sure what is going on but there is hardly a soul about."

Carrie's heart sank, for she knew exactly where everyone was, working themselves up into a frenzy before they marched on Marlborough Mill.

Without Margaret's influence though, Mr Thornton would surely stay in the house where it was safe while the soldiers handled the rioters. But things had already changed because Margaret had not seen Mr Thornton when she visited the mill. What if he was caught in the yard this time? Or if the rioters managed to break into the mill and attack the Irish workers hiding in there?

"Margaret, I think you should return to the mill; I think we need to warn Mr Thornton."

"About what?" Margaret asked, confused by her statement.

"I think that the workers are about to attack the mill."

"Whatever for?"

"Did you not see faces in the mill window while you were there?"

"I saw no one but Williams and Mrs Thornton."

"Well Mr Thornton has brought Irish workers over and the strikers aren't happy. They're going to start a riot." Her voice was rising with panic and Margaret was starting to give her strange looks.

"I hardly think that is likely, Carrie. Mr Higgins has stated time and again that this is to be a peaceful protest and that there will be no violence."

"Can't you just take my word for it?" Carrie asked. "Please."

Margaret looked indecisive for a moment and Carrie thought that she might be able to persuade her to return to the mill but just then Mrs Hale called for her daughter.

"I must go to my mother."

Carrie sighed. With no other option, she grabbed a shawl and headed out, running most of the way to the mill. The streets were quiet, eerily quiet but thankfully she reached Marlborough Mill without incident and knocked on the gates. Williams, the overlooker, let her in.

"Where's Mr Thornton?" she asked.

"You'd best wait in t'ouse, Miss, I'll find Mr Thornton."

"No, you don't understand. I think the strikers are coming. They know about Mr Thornton's Irish workers and they're going to attack the mill."

Williams paled but nodded.

"Get in t'ouse, Miss. I'll tell t'master."

"No, we need to barricade the gates!" she argued.

"They're locked," he assured her, but Carrie knew they would give away to the strikers eventually.

"Fine, you go and find Mr Thornton, I'll stay with Mrs Thornton," she said, taking two steps towards the house but when Williams ran into the mill, Carrie turned and headed back towards the gate.

There was a cart not far away, loaded with cotton bales. She thought that if she could move it in front of the gates, it might shore them up for a while.

Thankfully, though it was heavy, the cart moved fairly easily and she managed to manoeuvre it sideways on to the gate so that it could not roll away when the gates struck it. She then placed stones in front of and behind each wheel to stop it moving easily and stepped back just in time to hear the roar of the crowd as it advanced on the mill. She backed away.

Suddenly she felt strong arms encircling her waist and she was lifted off her feet and carried into Mr Thornton's house.

Chapter Eight

"Put me down!" Carrie cried and finally Mr Thornton set her back on her feet and locked the front door behind them.

"What were you thinking, placing yourself in danger like that?" He sounded angry.

"I was thinking that I didn't want anything to happen to you or your mill. Besides, I had plenty of time to accomplish my task."

"Foolish woman!" he said, dashing a hand through his hair.

"You'd better go and check on your mother," Carrie said. When he left she made her way into the front parlour and watched the crowds as they pushed against the gate. "Come on," she said under her breath, willing the soldiers to arrive before the gates gave way.

Mr Thornton returned a moment later.

"You should step away from the window," he said. "Mother and Fanny are at the back of the house; it's safest back there."

"No, I want to see what's happening."

"Don't you ever think about your own safety?" he almost shouted. "What if they were to throw a brick at the window?"

"They haven't broken through the gate yet, they're too far away."

How wrong could a person be, she wondered a few moments later as a stone hurtled towards the window. She just had time to push John out of the way and turn her back but as the shattered glass washed over her, she could feel a piece of it slice into her upper arm. She had no time to think about that however since Mr Thornton was lying on the ground, unmoving.

"Oh God!" she cried, rushing to his side. She heard the whistles from the soldiers when they arrived and the cries as the rioters began falling under their attack but she paid them no attention because Mr Thornton's head was bleeding where it had impacted with a table. Her attempt to save him might well have killed him!

"Come on, Mr Thornton, wake up!" she called, tapping his cheek.

When he refused to rouse she cried out for help and moments later Mrs Thornton, Fanny and two maids entered to see her kneeling over his body, cupping his face.

"Please, John, you can't die! Wake up."

"Fetch the doctor," Mrs Thornton said to Jane, one of the maids. Although she was just as concerned for her son as Carrie was, she had years more practice at controlling her emotions.

"But the rioters!" Jane protested.

"Fine." Unwilling to wait a moment longer than necessary, Mrs Thornton could see that she was the only one brave enough to summon the help her son needed and she left without another word.

"Help me get him to the sofa," Carrie said and the two maids ran forward to assist her. Fanny was talking nonsense, wondering what would happen to them all if John died but Carrie couldn't think about that yet.

"Do you have any ice?" she asked one of the maids.

"Ice?"

"Yes, you know, frozen water."

"No ma'am."

"Then get me a cloth and the coldest water you can find." Jane just looked at her as though she had spoken in a foreign language. "Now!" Carrie barked, and Jane scurried away.

Carrie parted Mr Thornton's hair to get a good look at the wound and tried to clean the blood up as best she could with his handkerchief. She knew that head wounds always bled a lot and so this might not be as serious as it looked. She held the handkerchief over the wound and applied pressure since there was little else she could do until Jane returned. Thankfully it wasn't long before the maid came back with a bowl of water and a small towel.

"I drew it fresh from t'well so its nice and cold," Jane said, placing the bowl and towel on the floor beside Carrie.

"Thank you." Carrie dipped the towel in the water, which was indeed very cold, and wiped the rest of the blood away. She rinsed the rag out a few times then pressed it over his wound. The cold should help lessen the swelling and stop the blood flow.

With little else to do, she sat by his side and took his hand in her free one, letting her tears fall unchecked.

"Okay, John, I know you can hear me. You can't leave me, okay? This is all my fault, I have messed everything up but you can't die because then I can never put things right! You... you don't know how much you mean to me." Her next words were so soft that only Jane was close enough to hear. "I love you."

Moments later John finally began to rouse and Carrie breathed a sigh of relief.

"Oh, thank god! How do you feel?" she asked.

"As though my head is about to explode."

She helped him sit up.

"What's your name?" she asked.

"What?" He sounded confused.

"Your name," she repeated firmly.

"John Thornton."

Carrie held up two fingers.

"How many fingers am I holding up?"

"Two."

"What year is it?"

"1855."

"And who is the prime minister." She suddenly realised that she had no idea herself who the prime minister was, rendering the question rather useless.

"Lord Palmerston."

"And the King?"

"It's *Queen* Victoria."

She smiled, pleased that he had caught her out.

"Do you mind telling me what the point of all this is?" he asked rather gruffly.

"Be quiet." She held up one finger. "Follow my finger with your eyes."

"But-"

"Just do it!"

She had no idea what to look for but he seemed to be focusing on her finger as it moved, which she was sure was a good thing. She looked into his eyes, searching for a blown pupil. She wasn't one hundred percent sure that was a sign of brain damage but thankfully he didn't have one anyway.

"How's your head?" she asked.

"Thick."

"Any double vision?"

"No."

"Do you feel tired?"

"I'd say more irritated right now."

"Good," she smiled, "I think that means you'll live but don't go to sleep for the next few hours and if you do start to feel drowsy..."

'What?' she asked herself as her words trailed off. *'Come and see me so I can drill a hole in your head and relieve the pressure?'*

"If you do feel drowsy, call Dr Donaldson and tell him."

"Very well," he snapped. "Are you done now?"

She felt stung by his harsh words, she had only been trying to make sure that he was okay.

"Yes," she said, her voice small.

"Good, now let me have a look at that bloody arm before I have to tie you down."

Carrie smiled slightly, her mood improving as she realised that his irritation had been caused by his concern for her.

"It is just a scratch," she assured him.

"Then let me see," he insisted.

Fanny and the maids were still standing around, watching the scene before them.

"Would someone fetch some me some lint, a bandage and some whisky," Carrie said as she tore the already ripped sleeve of her dress to reveal the cut.

She knew it was deeper than a simple cut and would probably need bandaging but it wasn't so deep that it would need stitches. Though it probably wasn't very sanitary, she rinsed the cloth she had been using on John and used it to clean her wound but John put his hands over hers and took the towel, then he gently began to cleanse the wound for her.

"This is no scratch," he admonished.

"Why do you think I asked for a bandage," she said with a smile.

Jane returned with the whisky and bandages. Carrie dipped a dry end of the cloth into the neck of the whisky bottle and upended it, then wiped the alcohol soaked rag over the wound. It stung slightly but not too badly.

"What are you doing?" John finally asked.

"Sterilising the wound. Alcohol kills bacteria."

"And bacteria are?"

"Things that cause infections. This is not exactly sterile but it's better than nothing." She said a silent thank you to her girl guide group for teaching her this kind of first aid stuff.

"Do you want to do the honours?" she asked, handing him the lint and bandage.

"I think you should see a doctor?"

"I don't need a doctor."

"I'd prefer it if you did."

"I'm fine!" she snapped. "Look, if I were at home I'd have just put superglue in the wound or some butterfly plasters over it but I'm not at home, I'm stuck here in a place I have no business being and I'm messing everything up! The Hales can't afford any more medical bills and besides, the doctors in this time don't even know that things have to be sterile and I'm damn well not going to land them with the cost of a treatment that ends up giving me blood poisoning!"

She regretted her outburst almost immediately but she couldn't take it back now.

"Hush," John placated her. "We will pay for a doctor."

"Ugh!" Carrie grabbed the lint from him and set about bandaging up her arm. Thankfully her sleeve was loose enough that she could pass the bandage around her arm without ripping the sleeve off completely. It was awkward but somehow she managed and Mr Thornton, realising that he wasn't going to win this argument, secured the bandage for her with a safety pin.

"There," she said with as much dignity as she

could muster. She rinsed the cloth out again and ran it over her face, wiping away the many tears that had dried there. "Now I really must get home. I'm afraid I left in something of a rush and the Hales might be worried about me."

"You shouldn't-" John's words were cut off with a harsh look from Carrie. Clearly she was still in no mood to be told what to do. "Let me see you home at least."

"You have a head injury; you shouldn't exert yourself."

Carrie stood up and realised that her sleeve was still badly torn and she had no idea where the shawl she had brought with her was. She had a vague memory of removing it when she manoeuvred the cart in front of the gates but there was no telling where it might be now.

"Can I borrow a shawl to hide my sleeve?"

"I will fetch you one," Fanny assured her and Jane accompanied her out of the room.

"Leave us," Mr Thornton said to Sarah, the other maid. "Will you not stay, at least for a while?" he asked Carrie.

"I shouldn't. I am too confused at the moment, I need some space to clear my head and think. I'm sorry."

She left the room and John didn't try to stop her. As she waited in the hall she could hear Fanny's words as she spoke to Jane on the landing above.

"Such a show to make of herself, and using his Christian name as well! And with witnesses there too! Mama said she had set her eye on John and this proves it!"

Oh no, she groaned. Now Mr Thornton would feel honour bound to propose to her and not Margaret. The longer she stayed in this time, the bigger mess she made of everything.

"Did you see what she did with that whisky! She is such a strange girl." Jane said.

"I know. Mother calls her wild, and can you blame her after witnessing what we just did! Why, no lady would ever behave in such a shameless manner."

Just then they rounded the top of the stairs and saw Carrie looking at them but she was too tired to get into another slanging match with Fanny. She simply accepted the shawl with a thank you and left.

Chapter Nine

Mrs Thornton was surprised to see Carrie climbing into a cab as she and Dr Donaldson arrived at the mill but she had more important things to worry about right now.

She breathed a sigh of relief when she entered the house to see John sitting on the sofa, awake though he was holding his head in his hands.

"John?" she called from the doorway.

He looked over at her and smiled slightly. Though he didn't think he needed a doctor, he allowed himself be examined since it would put his mothers mind at rest. Unlike Carrie's extensive and strange questions, the doctor just looked at him, prodded the cut on his head, took his pulse and said that it looked worse than it was.

He wondered at the strange things Carrie had been doing and saying. What did the name of the Queen have to do with anything? She was such an enigma, speaking riddles and nonsense but whatever she was talking about, she seemed certain. What did she mean by sterilising her cut with whisky? Making it barren? Barren from what? Bacteria? What was a bacteria?

She had spoken of this time as if it wasn't her time but didn't everyone share time? It seemed pretty universal to him.

He was vaguely aware of his sister relating the shocking series of events to his mother but he paid her no heed. He thought he remembered Carrie saying that she loved him and yet she kept insisting that she was not the one for him. What did that even mean?

He tried not to think about it but the idea that she

might be insane kept plaguing him. He didn't want to believe it, for she was so efficient and logical and yet she was also highly emotional, more so than most women he knew, and she kept talking rubbish as though he should understand what she meant.

His head was beginning to throb and he sighed deeply.

"How are you?" His mother asked him.

"I'm fine, Mother, just..." he didn't know what he was.

Well, that wasn't strictly true, he did know that he was in love, or at least he was as certain as a man can be. What he didn't know was if the woman he loved was a lunatic or a prophet.

The police came and spoke to Mr Thornton and Williams in the hope of getting as many names of the rioters as possible. Mr Thornton didn't tell them that Carrie had been present because he knew that she didn't want to worry the Hales but even if she hadn't said anything, he would have felt too bad about the police turning up on their doorstep while Mrs Hale was so ill to give them Carrie's name. A sharp look to Williams when the officers asked if there was anyone else present was enough to convey to his overlooker than Carrie was to be left out of this.

He spoke with the police for a long while and went with them as they surveyed the damage for their report. He then set about arranging for the mill gate to be repaired and the parlour window replaced. Thanks to Carrie's idea of setting the wagon in front of the gates, by the time the rioters broke through it they hadn't had enough time to do much damage before the soldiers arrived.

Finally he returned to the house and poured himself a finger of brandy and sat in one of the arm chairs in the front parlour. The broken window, now boarded up, only served as a reminder of what had happened earlier. He could feel his mother and sister both watching him anxiously but he paid them no mind.

He finished his drink and stood up.

"Where are you going?" Mrs Thornton asked.

"To see if Miss Preston is well."

"Don't," his mother admonished.

"Why? Is it too late to disturb them?"

"It is late for Mrs Hale," his mother answered. "She is unwell, remember?"

John nodded though clearly he still wanted to go.

"I must check... Miss Preston..."

"She looked well enough when I saw her leave," Mrs Thornton assured him.

"She was injured. I heard Fanny tell you that she cut her arm."

"She is such a reckless young woman." Mrs Thornton rolled her eyes.

John headed towards the door.

"I am sure she is well," His mother called. "It's you I am more concerned about."

"I'm fine, mother."

"John!"

He stopped and turned back to her.

"I'm asking you not to go."

John looked at her for a long while. Hannah Thornton wasn't usually one to make demands on her son and so the few times when she did, he usually listened. She was his mother after all and he owed her a lot.

"You have my word," he said, but he still needed to get out of the house for a while. He turned and left.

***

When Carrie arrived back at the Hales she went straight to her bedroom and removed her dress. She examined her arm and was pleased to note that while some blood had seeped through the lint and bandage, it wasn't much; the bleeding was stopping. Her sleeve was badly damaged but she might be able to do something to hide the repair. She got a similar dress out of her wardrobe but she wasn't ready to get dressed again yet. She hung the dress on the wardrobe door and went over to her bed.

She curled up on top of the covers and began to cry silently as the events of the day caught up with her.

Everything was wrong! Trying to fix things had only made everything worse and now after her hysterical display earlier, John would surely feel compelled to ask for her hand in marriage.

She had to get away, she had to go home before she destroyed everything, but how?

She cried for a long while until eventually Margaret found her. She sat on the side of the bed and asked what was wrong but Carrie was either unable or unwilling to tell her, so Margaret simply lay down behind her, put her arm around her waist and comforted her as best she could.

John was out for most of the evening as he walked, trying to understand the enigma that he was so desperately in love with. At one point he found himself on the hillside where they had talked about the kind of people they wanted to be.

He couldn't believe her mad. Mistaken; misguided perhaps but not mad. He believed that he had seen her heart that day and it was pure and untouched by insanity.

That left him where he was before, in love with a

woman he didn't understand.

Finally as the hour neared midnight he had little choice but to head back towards the mill.

"Are you still up?" he asked his mother as he came in to the parlour, surprised to find that she hadn't retired to bed.

"Where have you been?" his mother asked, doing her best to keep her voice even.

"Just walking."

"Where have you been walking?"

"I promised you I would not go there and I did not."

"But?"

"But I intend to go there tomorrow and I think you know what I intend to say."

"Yes, I do. You could hardly do otherwise."

"What do you mean?"

"I mean that after allowing her feelings to overcome her earlier, you are bound in honour. After the show she made of herself today you could hardly do anything else. The servants saw, you know. I'm sure her outrageous behaviour is already the talk of Milton."

"Bound in honour? Mother, I will ask for her hand because I love her, not because I have any desire to save her reputation!"

"Do not be angry with me, John." He was standing behind her chair so she put her embroidery down and stood up. She reached a hand up and cupped his cheek. "She has shown her feelings for all the world to see and I'm sure she will take you from me, that is why I did not want you to go. After tonight, I will stand second. I wanted you to myself, all to myself, for a few hours longer, that is why I begged you not to go there tonight."

Touched by her words and encouragement, John

leaned forward and kissed her cheek.

"You do not want to try to talk me out of it?" he asked softly, for she had made a few comments in the past that gave him reason to believe that she thought Miss Preston an unsuitable wife for him.

"Even if I could, I wouldn't. You are your own man, John, and I am proud of the man you have become. For all her faults, if she is the one you want I will support you. I will always support you."

"Thank you, Mother."

Fearing a visit from Mr Thornton, the next day Carrie took herself out early. She walked hills and streets that she did not normally visit, although she was careful to keep away from the less salubrious areas of town.

Yesterday's violence had brought the strike to an end and Milton was back at work, the streets once again bustled with the industry that had been sadly lacking in the past few weeks.

She managed to keep herself busy until five o'clock, when she felt that she had no choice but to return home. She told the Hales that she had a headache and, taking a book with her for company, she headed to bed for the rest of the evening. She knew they would never disturb her, even for Mr Thornton but each time there was a knock at the door, she held her breath.

She intended to follow a similar plan the next day but as she left the house the following morning, Mr Thornton was crossing the street to meet her.

Carrie took a deep breath to try to prepare herself for what was about to come. Mr Thornton's features were set and he looked determined as he crossed the street and stopped a short distance in front of her.

"Miss Preston, I see you are off for another all

day walk," he said, naturally falling into step beside her as by unspoken consent, they began walking.

"Yes, I lost track of time yesterday." She knew it was a poor excuse but telling him the truth, that she had been avoiding him, would have been cruel.

"And evidently made yourself unwell," he noted.

"It was nothing."

"As I suspected." He said with a wry smile, confirming her suspicion that he had easily seen through her excuse.

They walked in silence until they entered the park; Carrie trying to think of a way to stop him from asking what she thought he wanted to, and Mr Thornton waiting until they were alone before broaching the subject he had come to discuss with her.

"Do you still wish to hide from me?" he asked as they wandered, neither of them particularly concerned about their destination.

"No, that was cowardly of me. However I think I know what you are about to say and I think you know that I must refuse."

"I know no such thing," he assured her.

"Mr Thornton... You are not destined to spend your life with me."

"So you have said before, and yet you never explain what you mean or how you could possibly know such a thing."

"Because you would not believe it if I did tell you and I would rather you think me foolish than crazy."

"If I am not meant for you, as you put it, then why do you even care what my opinion of you is?"

"Vanity, I suppose. You... you are something of a hero to me, Mr Thornton, and although I cannot have you, I should still hate for you to think badly of me."

"I could never think ill of you, Carrie."

"Mr Thornton, I don't think it is proper for you to use my first name."

"As you used mine yesterday?" he countered.

"I was... distressed."

"Because you love me and you were worried about me."

She was about to deny it but the words wouldn't come.

"Yes," she finally admitted in a small voice.

"You admit that and yet continue to refuse me?"

"Because-"

"Because you are not meant for me!" he snapped. "And what of what I want? Does that count for nothing?"

"No! I mean... Oh, don't confuse me."

"Confuse you!" he snorted. "I rather think it is you who spouts absurdities that you refuse to explain."

"Then why would you even want someone as reckless, wild and baffling as me?"

"Why?" he grabbed her arm and spun her to face him, placing his hands on her shoulders to hold her still. "Because I love you, you foolish woman! Can you not understand that?"

He looked genuinely pained and Carrie felt tears prick her eyes.

"Will you not even try and explain your reasoning to me?" he asked and Carrie was surprised to see tears shining in his eyes.

They stood there, seemingly frozen in time for a moment, until suddenly he released her and turned to walk quickly away.

Carrie watched him go, almost hoping that he would look back but he didn't. She knew how deeply she had hurt him but she was unable to see any way to change it. She stayed in the park for a few minutes longer and then headed home, taking her time as she walked the streets of Milton, using the hustle and bustle around her to keep her mind off recent events.

Back at the house she turned to her usual distraction of books. She didn't have the same selection here that was available in her time but she managed to find a copy of Persuasion which she buried her head in for the rest of the day.

That evening a letter arrived for Carrie from Mr Thornton. She dreaded opening it, fearing his reproachful words, but he simply reprimanded her for not returning to work and stated that he expected her there at nine the following morning.

Carrie pondered her choice for the rest of the evening but in the end she knew that she would return to work. She told herself that it was because the Hales needed the money but the truth was that she couldn't live without seeing him. He had become like oxygen to her, vital to her survival and she could no more turn him down that she could have cut off her own arm.

Chapter Ten

The next few weeks proved to be a torment to both Carrie and Mr Thornton.

As though determined to prove himself over her, Mr Thornton spoke to her only when he had to and never looked at her unless absolutely necessary. Carrie did her work to the best of her ability and left, breathing a sigh of relief each day to leave his stifling presence behind her and yet even moments after she had left, inexplicably looking forward to seeing him again the next day.

Mr Thornton took every opportunity to visit the house, showing Mrs Hale the utmost care and concern during his visits and often bringing her gifts of fresh fruit or flowers.

Again, he rarely spoke to Carrie or even looked at her while he was there but he seemed to go out of his way to be solicitous to Margaret.

Though this was what she wanted, what must happen, what was destined to happen, it broke Carrie's heart to witness it.

As expected, poor Bessy Higgins died and Mr Higgins became a frequent visitor to the house as he talked with Mr Hale about his grief and many other matters. Carrie enjoyed these talks because Mr Higgins was passionate about the subjects that they discussed and she found it easy to get distracted by his persuasive arguments.

At work though, Carrie's torment seemed endless and some days she even wondered if she was doing the right thing by staying in Milton. Without independent means though, she had little choice. She often spoke to her aunt when she was alone, though sadly her aunt could no longer offer her the wisdom that she had shown when she was alive.

One afternoon Carrie was lying on her bed, staring at the ceiling above her, but at least she wasn't crying for a change. When Margaret entered their room unexpectedly she sighed as she saw Carrie and sat down next to her.

"Will you not tell me what troubles you so?" she asked. "Every day I see you looking more and more miserable and I only wish there was something I could do to help you."

"There's nothing anyone can do." Carrie said.

"How do you know unless you tell me?"

Carrie didn't reply.

"Is it your family?" Margaret asked.

"I do miss them," she confessed. Lately she had often been getting their picture out of her purse and staring at it. Truth be told it wasn't so much them that she missed, but the familiar. Everything here was so different, so backwards! Her only solace during her predicament had been Mr Thornton, and now even he seemed to hate her. "But it is not that." She admitted as she looked at Margaret. "There is someone I like very much but I cannot have him."

"You are heartsick," Margaret sympathised, for although she had not experienced it herself, she had often read about how painful lost love could be.

"I suppose." Carrie had never heard it called that but it wasn't a bad description.

"He does not love you?" Margaret asked.

"No, I believe he does but he is not mine to have."

"I'm sorry," Margaret took Carrie's hand, assuming that the man she loved was betrothed to another. It wasn't uncommon for men to marry for money, forsaking the women they truly loved in the process.

"It's not your fault," Carrie said.

"Perhaps not, but you have been so good to my family and especially my father, that it pains me to think of you being unhappy, no matter what the cause."

Carrie wiped her eyes and tried to smile.

"Thank you."

Margaret smiled back.

"Do you know, I thought for a time that you might like Mr Thornton."

Carrie's eyes shot to Margaret's and she looked frightened, as if she had been caught.

"It is Mr Thornton? But he is not engaged, is he?"

"No, not exactly. It's complicated."

"I'm sure, but... well does someone else have a prior claim on him?"

"Yes, I suppose."

"Someone we know?"

This was getting a little too close for comfort so Carrie didn't answer.

"Well, you are far too good for the likes of him, anyway," Margaret said, trying to comfort her in some small way.

"You still don't like Mr Thornton then?" Carrie asked, for surely Margaret should be warming to him by now.

"I do not dislike him as such, but I do not particularly like him either. He has been very kind to my mother, and I know how much Father values his lessons with Mr Thornton. For those reasons I am pleasant to him but I cannot claim to like him."

"Because he is a manufacturer?"

"No, because he is rather rough. His ways are not our ways and I find them very unappealing."

Carrie sighed, for it was starting to seem that she had no hope of getting Margaret to ever like

Mr Thornton.

The next week Carrie saw a poster for a circus that was coming to Milton and her eye was caught by one of the other attractions that would be there, namely psychic readings by Lilith.

Her Aunt Imelda had loved psychics and had believed in them, through she freely admitted that many were charlatans.

Despite having no luck wishing herself home, Carrie was unable to forget the letter Aunt Imm had written and how she spoke about the earrings giving Carrie her heart's desire. Was it possible that something mystical was happening here? Or was this all just one big long dream, in which case she really should throw herself at Mr Thornton, for no harm could come from a dream.

She resolved to go and see the psychic while the circus was in town. It might be a waste of time but if there was even the slightest hope of understanding what was happening to her, she would take it.

Chapter Eleven

The day before the circus arrived in town, Frederick Hale came to see his mother and the whole house went into lockdown.

When he joined the navy, the family had high hopes for Fred, Mr Hale especially, believing that it would be the making of him. Unfortunately when he joined another ship, his new captain turned out to be a tyrant who beat and abused his crew. During one such beating it looked as if the captain would kill the young deck hand, still only a child and, sickened by what he saw, Fred felt he had no choice but to step in. With few options at their disposal, he and a handful of the other officers set the captain and those officers who were still loyal to him afloat on a life raft.

The Navy called it a mutiny and hanged those it could capture. Fred fled the country and finally settled in Spain, living under an assumed name.

Though there was still a sizeable price on his head, when Mrs Hale had asked to see her only son one last time, Margaret had felt compelled to write to her brother and, being the good and loving son that he was, Fred had felt duty bound to take the risk and return to see his mother one last time.

Carrie was basically the only one allowed out of the house for her work, and then only so that she could pick up anything else they needed on her way home. She also went to see Mr Hale's pupils to tell them that he was ill and would not be able to give them their lessons this week.

That seemed to keep most people away and Carrie spent much of her time at home, reading on her own so as to give the family time together.

On the third day of Frederick's visit, Carrie had no errands to run on her way home, so she decided to go straight to the circus from work, thinking that it would be quieter in the afternoon and that she might have longer to speak with the psychic.

Lilith worked from a small tent outside the main circus marquee and charged two pence per reading. In the event though, her small tent was closed and a sign hanging outside proclaimed it would not open for another two hours, so Carrie stood and waited.

"Won't open for a while, love," a young lady said she she passed. "You'd best come back later."

"I'm happy to wait, thank you."

"Somethin' important, is it?"

"I suppose."

"But you won't tell me what it is," the other woman guessed. She was dressed simply, in a functional brown skirt and white blouse, her long red hair plaited down her back.

"No, I'm sorry."

"Don't be, we're used to sceptics round 'ere. Why don't you come with me and we'll see if we can't get Lilith to see you a bit earlier."

"Oh, I don't want to put her to any trouble."

"Don't worry, Lilith always wants paying customers. Follow me, love."

She led Carrie through the small wooden caravans and tents until she arrived at a wooden caravan with 'Lilith's Psychic Readings' painted on the side. The woman climbed into the rear of the caravan and Carrie paused, unwilling to enter without an invitation.

"Are you comin'?" the woman called, so Carrie mounted the wooden steps and found that the woman she had been speaking with was the only one in there and she was seated at a table.

"You're Lilith?"

"I am," she smiled and gestured to a Romany looking outfit hanging on the wall. "I look more the part once me stall opens, it's what the folks expect. Who might you be?"

"I'm Carrie."

Lilith held her hand out and shook Carrie's.

"Sit yourself down, lass, and let's see what we can do for you."

Carrie sat opposite her and Lilith reached out and took her hand, then closed her eyes.

"You are a long way from home," she said.

Well, Carrie's accent was proof of that.

"But it's more than just distance, you have come from much further away. You feel lost, though you are exactly where you are supposed to be."

Lilith suddenly opened her eyes and dropped Carrie hand as though she'd been scolded.

"Why are you here?" Lilith asked, her tone sharp.

"I want you to contact someone for me, someone who's dead."

"You think this person has the answers you seek?"

"How do you know I'm seeking answers?"

"Because everyone who comes to see me wants answers, but I'm sorry, I cannot contact the dead. I can only see the past and the future."

"So what do you see in my future?" Carrie asked. Lilith's sudden withdrawal was worrying.

"I saw..." Lilith licked her lips. "I saw a family. You will have many children and die an old lady."

"Oh, don't talk bollocks!" Carrie snapped. "I know you saw something and I know it wasn't nice."

Lilith looked slightly taken aback by her sharp words.

"People who come to me don't want the truth," she told Carrie. "They want reassurance."

"Well I don't," Carrie assured her. "I need to know if I'm ever going to get home."

"No," Lilith said with surety. "The place you call home is not something I recognise, but I know that you are destined never to see it again."

"Why?"

"Because you made a choice, you asked Fate to change the hand that you'd been dealt and Fate intervened. Your destiny has changed but Fate does not offer second chances. In fact I have only once heard of Fate being harnessed in such a way and it takes a very powerful sorcerer to do it. Way out of my league."

"Okay." Carrie took some deep calming breaths and tried to blink back the tears that threatened to fall. She had already guessed that she was stuck here but hearing it confirmed brought her emotions to the surface. Though they had argued a lot and weren't very close, she missed her family and the idea of never seeing them again was a difficult reality to come to terms with.

Still, she reasoned, many people lost their families, at least she had the comfort of knowing that her's were alive and well.

"Okay, so if I am stuck here, I need to know if I made the right decision about something."

Lilith's expression turned compassionate.

"No," she said softly. "In refusing him you have condemned yourself and those around you to misery."

"Why should I believe you?" Carrie asked.

"You have no reason to trust me, but then I have no reason to lie."

Carrie looked into the eyes of the woman

opposite her and could see no signs of deception.

"And what would have happened if I'd said yes?" Carrie asked, her voice soft and fearful.

"It's not very clear but, though different to what life had originally planned for you, you would have been happy, much happier than Fate originally intended."

"And what about Margaret? If I had said yes, what would have happened to her?"

"She would have married a politician."

"But is she happy?"

"She would have been, yes."

"What have I done?" Carrie felt her tears spill over.

Lilith reached out again and took her hand, but this time to offer comfort rather than gain insight.

"The fact that I can see anything of an alternate future means that you still have time. It is not too late."

"Really?"

"Yes."

Carrie smiled.

"I must offer you a word of caution though. Be truthful with him, absolutely truthful about everything. If you try and hide who you really are, your marriage will be built on lies and distrust is the only possible outcome."

"But he'll think I'm crazy."

"Perhaps, but do you really have so little faith in him?"

Carrie sniffed and got her handkerchief out to wipe her eyes.

"I suppose not. Well, the truth is I idolise him."

Lilith smiled and got up to make some tea. Carrie got her purse out.

"No, just tell me the truth about where you're

from," Lilith said, refusing the money. "I have never seen any place like it before."

"Well..." She thought she might as well get some practice in now. Besides, what did it matter if Lilith thought she was crazy since she was probably never going to see her again. "I'm from the future."

Lilith stared at her for a long time before she slowly nodded.

"Aye, I believe you are." She smiled. "And how did you come to be here?"

"I'm not quite sure. I think... My aunt died and left me some earrings that she said would give me my heart's desire, that's all I can think of."

"Those earrings?" Lilith asked, pointing to the ones she was wearing.

"Yes."

"May I?" Lilith reached out to touch them so Carrie took one earring off and handed it to her. Lilith inhaled sharply as she touched it. "Powerful magic indeed." She handed it back and returned to the table with a tea pot and two cups.

"But they can't get me back home?" Carrie asked, putting her earring back on.

"No. Like I said, no matter how powerful a sorcerer is, Fate can only be altered once, you can't reverse what's been done."

"The really strange thing though..." Carrie began, cupping her tea cup in her hands and staring into it's depths. "Well, where I'm from, this universe isn't real. The life I'm living, the people I'm meeting, they're all characters from a novel; just an invented story. How can I be living in fiction?"

"Is it fiction?" Lilith asked. "Me Mam used to say that the possibilities of the mind were endless. If we could dream it, then it was true."

Carrie thought about the the theory of multiple

dimensions and suddenly wished she'd paid more attention to those physics documentaries on the BBC. Was it possible that just dreaming something could create it? There was no denying that she seemed to be living her life in this fictional world so it must be possible. Did that mean that somewhere out there, there was a universe in which Harry Potter was real too?

She smiled at the thought but quickly sobered up again.

"What about my family?" she asked. "Back home, I mean. Will they... Will they miss me?"

"I don't know," Lilith answered truthfully. "Maybe when you left they forgot about you, as though you never existed in that world... or maybe they don't know what happened to you, and maybe they're searching."

"But there's nothing I can do for them, is there?"

"No, love. For better or worse, you're here now. You'd best make the most of it."

Carrie nodded and sipped her tea.

"Thank you, you've been, a big help."

"It's nice to use me gift for someone who really wants help for a change," Lilith smiled. "Most people just want to hear that they're going to meet a tall, dark, handsome stranger, or that they're going to die of old age. Now, drink up and then go and see about putting your mistake right, before anyone else suffers for it."

Carrie quickly finished her tea then returned to the mill yard. Now that she had made a decision, she was eager to see it through. She almost ran through the yard, into the offices and burst straight into Mr Thonrton's office without knocking.

Chapter Twelve

Mr Thornton looked up from his desk to see Carrie standing in his doorway. He knew that he should fire her and end this daily torment that they both endured but he couldn't bring himself to sever their working relationship because right now, it was the only relationship they had.

"Miss Preston, I thought you had left for the day." Though his words were pleasant, his tone was cold and hard.

"I had." Now that's she was here, her courage was failing her. "I... I need to talk to you, Mr Thornton. I want to tell you the truth about me, where I'm from and how I came to be here and if, after you've heard what I have to say, you would like to ask me to marry you again, I won't say no."

"If?" he asked.

"Yes, *if*." She swallowed down her panic at the idea that he might reject her. "Is there somewhere private where we can talk? Alone?"

"Will here not do?" he asked, for they were alone in his office.

"Yes, I suppose." She looked up into his eyes which were still cool and unfeeling. "There are some things I have to collect first though, things I need to show you. Will you wait for me?"

He glared at her for a moment, seemingly fighting his own judgement, then he turned away.

"Go," he told her, his back to her as he looked out across the mill courtyard.

"I won't be long," she assured him, retreating to the door.

Mr Thornton watched as she crossed the yard and left through the mill gate.

The idea that he might finally understand her thrilled him but at the same time he still felt the sting of her rejection most keenly. He was tempted to turn her away when she returned, though in his heart he knew that he couldn't. For better or worse, he was a fool in love and little more than a slave to his feelings for her.

Carrie borrowed a large basket from Dixon then went up to her room, putting her rucksack and handbag into the basket and covering them with a cloth, for such unusual items would surely draw attention if she made no effort to hide them. The family were all in Mrs Hale's room so she didn't face any awkward questions as she flew out of the house again and rushed back to the mill, eager to get this off her chest once and for all.

She looked to his office as she came back into the yard and was surprised to see him still standing at the window. She wondered if he had moved since she left. She tried to smile at him but she was nervous and it came out more like a grimace. She hurried inside instead.

He didn't turn to her as she entered and Carrie locked the door behind her so that they wouldn't be disturbed, then she picked her skirts up and sat down in the middle of the floor. Finally he turned to her, surprised to see her sitting on his floor.

She gestured to the space beside her and for possibly the first time since he was a child, Mr Thornton sat down on the floor.

"So, are you finally going to be honest with me?" he asked, his words sounding harsher than he meant them to.

"Yes, but there are some things I want to show you first." She got her handbag out of the basket and took her purse out. She pulled the picture of her family out and handed it to him.

"What is this?"

"A photograph of my family."

"Photographs aren't in colour. And their clothes are very strange."

"They are in colour where I'm from and as you can see, it isn't on a glass or copper plate either, just paper. That's my mother," she pointed. "That's my father and my sister and me when I was 12."

"What about your brother?"

"I don't have a brother. I lied."

He handed the picture back to her and Margaret got her college ID and driving license out, both of which had colour pictures of her on them. He looked at them closely then handed them back.

"You wear paint," he said, slightly disdainfully.

"Everyone does where I am from. Even some men." He looked sharply at her and she laughed slightly hysterically. "It's true, I'll show you."

She got her blackberry out and turned it on. She had turned it off almost as soon as she got here to save the battery so it had plenty of life left.

"This is a phone," she explained. "It's a bit like a telegram, but you can speak to the person on the other end. They also do all kinds of other things now, technology has moved on a lot."

She searched through her music file until she found the album cover of one of her favourite bands. She showed him the picture.

"Men in paint!" he said softly.

"They're one of my favourite bands. Musicians," she clarified.

"They play music?"

"And write it. Here," she took the phone back and played a song from the album. She opted for one of the slower singles but it was still very different from anything Mr Thornton was used to.

Mr Thornton jumped as the music began and after listening for minute or so, she stopped it.

"You call that music?"

"I do. A lot has changed where I come from."

She next pulled a book out of her rucksack, English Literature in Context, and opened it to the copyright page.

"Look at the publication date," she told him.

"2010?"

"It was published one hundred and fifty five years in the future."

"This is absurd."

"Is it?"

She next got her laptop out of the rucksack and turned it on.

"Where I come from we have something called electricity which powers all kinds of fancy machines. This is a computer."

"It looks like a typographer."

"It can be used as one, among other things."

Once it had booted up, she opened Microsoft Word and began typing, *'Hello, my name is Carrie Preston and I am from the 21st century'*.

"I write my essays on this for university. I'm taking a degree in English Literature."

Mr Thornton watched as the words she typed appeared on screen.

"It can do a lot of other things too," she said. "I can store music on here, I have some ebooks on here, which are novels in a format that can be read off this screen rather than in a printed book. I can store my photos on here." She opened up the file labelled personal pics so that she could see the thumbnails, then opened a picture of her with her sister. "There's also something where I come from called moving pictures or films." She opened another file and played one of her music videos, watching as Mr Thornton got closer to the screen while the video played.

"What are they doing?"

"Dancing."

"Doesn't look like any kind of dancing I've ever seen."

"It's street dancing."

She closed the window.

"The thing is, I know how crazy this sounds but I'm from the future," she explained, managing to only cringe slightly as she said the words. "My aunt granted me my heart's desire and somehow I ended up here and the reason I said that you are destined to be with someone else is because your future is my past. I've read about who you're supposed to marry."

Mr Thornton didn't answer her for a moment. Her toys were very clever but he had something more pressing on his mind at the moment.

"What's that," he asked, pointing to a thumbnail in her picture album. "Can you make it bigger like you did with the other one?"

Carrie opened the picture, though she dreaded his reaction to it. Mark was standing behind her, his arms around her waist as he kissed her cheek over her shoulder. Carrie was laughing.

"That's me at the Student Union's Halloween party last year. It's customary where I come from to dress up as someone else on Halloween, I went as a sexy nurse."

"And that man with his arms around you?"

"He's dressed as Cary Grant, he's an actor who made a lot of films."

"And who is he?"

"Mark. He was... my boyfriend."

Mr Thornton's features turned positively fierce as he glared at the screen.

"Things are very different where I come from," Carrie tried to explain. "People are free to show their affection to each other in public and fashions have changed drastically. It... it's not better or worse, just different."

"I have never seen a nurse look like that."

"No, well like I said, things are very different. Short skirts like that will become popular in the 1960's."

"You look very happy."

"I was having a good time. Celebrations and parties are much more jovial things where I come from, very informal."

"Is that man why you refused me?"

"What? God no! I was going to break up with him but then my aunt died and the next thing I knew, I was here so I didn't have a chance, but we were over, I promise you."

She cupped his face in her hands and turned him to look at her.

"I love you, not him."

She leaned forward and kissed him but he took hold of her shoulders and pushed her away, hard. She fell backwards and looked up at him as though she was seeing him for the first time.

"You expect me to have anything to do with a woman who behaves like that?" he asked, pointing to the laptop screen. "Cavorting, practically naked in public? You disgust me."

Carrie felt as though she had been punched in the solar plexus and physically couldn't catch her breath for a moment. She had heard of a broken heart but she had never believed that the pain could be this acute.

She stumbled to her feet, feeling disoriented and out of sorts, and ran for the door. She pulled on the handle for a few moments, frustrated that it wouldn't open until she remembered that she had locked it. She finally got it open and ran, her tears blinding her so that she was unable to navigate around people and was forced to push them out of the way.

She ran all the way home, making something of a spectacle of herself, and once home she ran up to her bedroom, threw herself down on the bed and sobbed until she was too tired to cry any more.

Mr Thornton watched her go, his heart was also breaking but he was unable to forgive her for loving another man. He leaned over the laptop and, though it took him a while to learn to use the mouse pad, he remembered how she had closed the previous photograph and he closed this one. He opened the next one. Carrie and Mark were dancing in this one, her arms around his shoulders.

He went from picture to picture. Each photograph of her and Mark was like a knife in his heart. She wasn't with Mark in all of them, in some she was alone, in some she was with other people and some photographs she wasn't in at all. Some of the people wore so few clothes that they were practically naked.

He had never witnessed such a wanton display of immorality before.

Then the photographs changed from the Halloween party. The next one showed Carrie sitting on a blanket on hillside, dressed in blue trousers and a knitted top. She seemed to be having a picnic with another girl. Her hair was loose and blowing in the wind. In the next picture she was smiling towards the camera against a backdrop of mountains, her face alight with pleasure. He had never seen her look so happy before. The pictures changed once again, this time to a dinner party. In the next she was with a group of friends. In the next she was sitting at a piano on stage. He wondered if she could play.

Then there came a cluster of pictures that seemed to be from another country since the buildings and plants were so unusual. Some pictures were just of buildings while others had Carrie and one or two other women in them. In many pictures they carried large bags on their backs and in all of them the girls were wearing trousers. The people in the background looked Asian.

The country obviously changed again as the other people in the photographs now had black skin, so perhaps she was in Africa or the Caribbean.

In the next picture she was a few years younger and sitting atop a horse but sitting astride it, not riding side saddle as was customary for ladies. She was smiling and there was a blue rosette pinned to her horse's bridle. In the next she was again astride a horse but wearing clothes much like his, including a top hat.

In the next she was in a field, feeding carrots to the chestnut horse and a black pony, her clothes were shabby and her boots filthy but she looked so happy. In the next she was grooming the chestnut horse, then seemingly mucking out its stall. That was no job for a lady! In the next photograph she was riding bareback with only a bridle on the horse. In the next she was jumping.

Then came a few pictures where she was wearing what looked like blue pyjamas with a green belt, but she seemed to be fighting in two of the pictures. In the third she was bowing to someone else.

In very few of the pictures was she painted and in none was she as painted as in the Halloween photographs. Perhaps she wasn't such a loose woman after all and painting one's face was something of a tradition on Halloween. After all, hadn't her... No, he couldn't bring himself to even think the word. After all, hadn't *'that man'* with her in the photograph also been painted?

He had run out of pictures so he closed the window only to see the file that she had played the moving pictures from. He opened another file and watched, fascinated as the people moved and spoke to each other.

The women were all dressed in form fitting clothes and trousers and the rules of society didn't seem to be kept to at all. Two men with unusual accents were speaking about a crime with a lady. Another man had been slain and the language they were using was quite vulgar to use in front of a woman. The men, however, seemed to be taking their orders from her; she was their boss!

The boss-woman had a third man with her but he seemed to be her friend rather than her employee, yet he still did what she said. They went to see some military people and he was shocked to note that some of the military people were women and they were dressed in exactly the same uniforms as the men!

Then there was a gun fight and the friend-man cowered while the boss-woman withdrew a very small gun and began shooting, protecting the man!

If this was where Carrie came from he could see that things were indeed very different. Suddenly the screen went black. He shook the machine a few times but it remained black. He had obviously broken her magic toy.

He leaned away from the laptop, surprised to realise that he had gotten so close to it in the first place, but he didn't get up off the floor. Instead he began going through the other items in her basket.

She had some other photographs in her purse, which was unlike any purse he had ever seen before; one picture of her with her horses and one of her father.

There were lots of printed scraps of paper detailing prices and the dates on all of these pieces of paper were 2011. She also had a number of strange coins, squares of something like card with bank names and long numbers on them and probably thirty or forty thousand pounds in diamonds stored in the same pocket as the coins! A diamond ring, a pendant, a brooch and earrings. Stones of this size just weren't seen outside of the aristocracy and those with immense wealth.

He looked at the coins which declared themselves to be 1, 2, 5, 20, 50 pence as well as 1 and 2 pound coins. Each coin was dated sometime between 1987 and 2009 and declared the Queen to be Elizabeth II rather than Victoria.

Next he took out the paper money, which were much smaller than the notes he was used to. He counted them up and she had nearly one hundred pounds in her purse! Of course it probably wasn't legal tender.

He looked through the rest of her handbag and found a date book for the year 2011, though it was labelled 'diary'. In the front was a folded timetable for classes at the University of London and she had slipped some letters in there as well. Though he knew better, he read them.

One was a handwritten letter from her father, postmarked Spain. The next was a letter from something called the National Health Service, whatever that was, telling her that she had to attend a pap smear test for cervical cancer. He wondered why anyone would test for cancer, for surely the growth itself was enough evidence that you had the disease? He wondered if Carrie did have this cervical cancer but forced that thought out of his mind, because the idea of losing her was too painful to contemplate.

But you've already lost her, a small voice in his head reminded him. He pushed that thought aside also.

Next he pulled out a box from her handbag that said *'Mates Variety. Natural, ultra thin, endurance and strawberry.'* He was still none the wiser to what the box contained so he turned it over and read the back. *'Mates Variety offers you a great selection of our best selling condoms'* what the hell is a condom, he thought. *'Natural for ultimate comfort, Ultra Thin for sheer pleasure, Endurance for longer lasting love making and Strawberry for a fruity feeling!'*

He read that last line again, just to be sure, but there was no mistaking the meaning of *'for longer lasting love making'* and he suddenly felt rather ill. She must have bought these for Mark. She and that horrible boy had...

He threw the packet away as though it had burned him. He couldn't believe that she would sleep with a man before marriage. There had been signs that she was forward, he supposed, such as when she winked at him, then hugged him, and one time she had kissed his cheek. And of course she hadn't thought ill of him when he had kissed her, but sex? No, he couldn't believe her capable of falling that low as to have relations outside of marriage. He reached out for the box, which said that there should be 12 of these condoms inside. He counted a second time to be sure but there was no mistaking the fact that only 10 condoms remained.

Chapter Thirteen

The next day was a Sunday. Though Fred was still here, Mr Hale and Margaret still went to church because not going would only cause people to worry and possibly call at the house to see how the family was. Carrie didn't feel like going today and told Mr Hale that she was feeling unwell. She roused herself enough to get dressed and allowed Dixon to do her hair, but only because Dixon seemed to take it as a personal affront when she did her own hair.

She had left all of her belongings from her old life with Mr Thornton. She knew she would have to get them back at some point but she couldn't face him just yet. Her computer and phone would probably have run out of battery by then, but she could hardly recharge them so it had to happen at some point.

She spent the day in a kind of dreamlike state, not quite in the present but not quite gone either. She drifted, doing as she was told and speaking only when she was spoken to.

Right now she missed her music even more than she missed her copy of North and South, for since Mr Thornton had broken her heart she found it difficult to be quite so enamoured of that story any longer. At home, whenever she was sad or angry or frustrated she would sit at her piano and play as loudly as she could, sometimes singing along and using it as a means to vent her feelings. Here though she had no such outlet.

Still, she found sad music running through her head, comforting her in a small way though it did nothing to help improve her mood.

The family ate lunch together and Carrie did her best to join in the conversation. The character of Fred had always interested her in the books and she wanted to get to know him a little better; she just didn't feel as though she had the energy to at the moment.

After lunch she sat by the window in the parlour, looking down at the street below, watching everyone as they went about their business. Since it was a Sunday their pace was much more leisurely today than usual. It was almost four o'clock when she saw Mr Thornton striding up the street towards the house, carrying the basket that she had left at the mill the day before.

Suddenly her body flooded with adrenalin. He must not be allowed in the house in case he saw Fred, but he also couldn't be left out on the street because she feared what would happen if someone else were to discover the things that he carried in the basket! She would be kidnapped and interrogated for her knowledge of the future or put into some insane asylum and left to rot, or her belongings stolen and used to enhance technology here early, causing Skynet to build Terminators and use them to wipe out humanity.

Okay, that probably wasn't the most objective reaction but it was hard to keep a level head when you had so many balls in the air at once.

She didn't know what to do for the best. She ran down the stairs, oblivious to the Hale's stares as she passed them, and opened the front door before Mr Thornton could knock.

She pulled him inside and manhandled him into the study which was just off the hallway.

"Such a greeting," he said, his voice as hard as iron as she closed the door behind them.

"I did not want you to disturb the Hales. Mrs Hale is very ill now."

"Or rather, you do not want them to learn what kind of woman you really are."

"Excuse me?"

Ignoring her, he pulled her essay file out of the basket and began to look through it.

"I don't understand it," he said. "This work is some of the finest I have ever seen. This essay, discussing the similarities between Robert Walton and Victor Frankenstein was so insightful; and this one on the depiction of Mr Bennet is so well argued that I could hardly believe that it was the work of a woman."

Carrie laughed at the irony.

"Those essays were written about arguably two of the best books in the history of the world. Both books were written by women and yet you question a woman's ability to analyse them?"

Clearly he didn't like being laughed at.

"Argue your way out of this one then." He reached into the basket once again and threw the packet of condoms at her. "Go on," he taunted. "Deny it!"

She caught the packet and blushed as she realised what they were.

"I have no intention of denying anything." This was no longer amusing and her back stiffened as he sat in judgement of her.

"So you admit it then; that you've debased yourself with that man in the photograph?"

Carrie stayed quiet, she had no intention of justifying herself to him.

"How many others have there been? How many others have you debauched yourself with? How many!"

"Fine, I'll tell you," she answered, her cool and calm attitude belying the rage she felt at his accusations.

"You will?" He seemed taken aback.

"Yes. I have done nothing that I am ashamed of."

"Go on then, tell me."

"I will. Just as soon as you tell me how many women you have slept with."

"What?"

"You heard me. You are a red blooded, thirty-something man, I hardly think it likely that you're still a virgin"

"That has got nothing to do with this."

"I think it has. If you want to sit in judgement of my behaviour, then I think I have a perfect right to sit in judgement of yours."

"That's different."

"Why? Because you're a man and I'm a woman?"

"Exactly."

"So I am expected to be pure and virginal on my wedding night, but I don't have the right to expect that from my husband?"

Mr Thornton looked uncomfortable.

"Well I'm sorry but I don't hold with double standards like that and where I come from, men and women are treated equally. So, if it really is that important for you to know exactly how many men I've slept with, then you'll have to tell me your magic number first."

Mr Thornton seemed to have been rendered speechless.

"Did you care about those women?" Carrie asked, taking advantage of his silence. "What were they, easy conquests? Innocent maids that you could take advantage of? Prostitutes? Did you even considering using protection to prevent pregnancy and infections?"

"You don't know what you're talking about." He was barely able to contain his anger but Carrie wasn't about to back down.

"On the contrary, I rather think I know a lot more about sex than you do. My culture has studied all aspects of sex, attraction and relationships. Where I come from most sexually transmitted diseases are easily curable and schools offer sex education classes, teaching teenagers what they need to know and how best to protect themselves against disease and unwanted pregnancy. Rather than examine sex, like my society, what has yours done? Told you that sex is bad, that sex is sinful, that you should only have sex after you're married. How's that working out, because it sure as hell doesn't look like that last one had any impact on you, did it, John?"

"Don't call me that."

"I'll call you whatever the hell I like. I opened my heart to you, *John*. I told you my biggest secret, something I haven't told anyone else since I arrived in this horrific, backwards time and you not only shove my gesture back in my face, you rip my heart out, stamp on it and now you think that you can come into my home and sit in judgement on me for a crime you are equally guilty of? Well I'm, sorry, but I'm not in the mood for hypocrisy today."

She opened the study door for him to see himself out and although he hesitated for a moment, he finally left. The front door slammed a few moments later and Carrie sagged against the study door frame as though her strings had been cut.

She looked over to the basket of possessions that had caused this mess and saw his gloves lying on the table beside it. Without thinking she picked them up and made to follow him out, but stopped just short of the front door. What was she thinking? He didn't deserve her thoughtfulness. In fact, he could rot in hell for all she cared.

"Are you all right?" She looked over to the bottom of the stairs, where Fred now stood. "We heard arguing. I wanted to come down but Father wouldn't let me until he was gone."

How was it that Fred, a virtual stranger, could be so kind while Mr Thornton, a man she would have done almost anything for, could be so cruel.

That thought was her undoing and she began to weep again.

"Oh, hey, it's all right."

Frederick came up to her and wrapped her in his embrace. There had never been a lot of tenderness in her life and she found herself unable to reject the comfort he offered. He tucked her head under his chin and stroked her back.

"Everything will work out for the best, you'll see," he told her.

But everything didn't work out for the best because at that precise moment, Mr Thornton returned for his gloves. She had meant to bolt the front door again but as she turned to look at him she realised that she had forgotten. Less than a second later she also realised that he had completely misread the situation that he had walked in on.

Mr Thornton took one look at Carrie in another man's arms and a red mist seemed to descend over him.

Carrie looked on in horror as he charged at Fred, knocking the younger man to the ground. They wrestled around on the floor, rolling over each other, both of them gaining the upper hand for a moment only to lose it again.

Mr Hale, Margaret and Dixon all came to see

what the commotion was but they were too shocked to make any move to break up the fight. Carrie was also shocked for a while, until she realised that if she didn't do something soon, one of these men was going to end up killing the other.

Mr Thornton gained the upper hand again and Carrie took the opportunity to pounce on his back. She wrapped her right arm around his neck, holding onto her left forearm with her other hand as she placed her left hand behind his head, pressing it forward.

He clawed at her arm, his nails raking painfully into her skin but he couldn't hold out for long against the wave of darkness that enveloped him and he soon became limp in her arms.

Knowing that she could cause brain damage if she held on for too long, she released him and with Fred's help, rolled him off the younger man. She offered Fred her hand and helped him up.

"What the hell did you do?" Fred asked.

"It's called a sleeper hold, it cuts off the blood flow to the brain. Hopefully he'll wake up in a few minutes."

"Help me get him up to the sitting room" Margaret said, coming down the stairs now that the danger had passed.

"Leave him there," Carrie said, for she was in no mood to be charitable

She was ignored however and between them, Fred, Dixon, Mr Hale and Margaret managed to get Mr Thornton upstairs and lay him out on the sofa there.

Dixon fetched some water and Margaret set about bathing Fred's injuries.

"What do we tell him when he wakes up?" Fred asked.

"I don't see that we have any alternative but to tell him the truth," Mr Hale said sounding resigned.

"But he's a magistrate," Margaret argued.

"He's an honourable man," Mr Hale said, ignoring Carrie's derisive snort. "I doubt that once he knows the whole story, he will betray us."

"I don't suppose we have much choice," Margaret agreed. "Why were you two fighting?" she asked Fred.

"It's not Fred's fault," Carrie hastened to defend him. "I was upset after Mr Thornton left and Fred was comforting me. I forgot to lock the door so when Mr Thornton returned for his gloves he saw us and became jealous. This is all my fault. I'm sorry."

"It's hardly your fault he walked in without knocking first," Mr Hale said kindly, for she certainly felt like she was to blame. "You cannot be held accountable for the actions of another."

"He must really like you," Fred said, trying to cheer Carrie up.

"He's got a funny way of showing it," she muttered.

"I'd best go and check on your mother," Mr Hale said, getting to his feet, although he looked very tired. "Make sure she wasn't disturbed."

"Do you want me to come?" Carrie asked.

"No, you stay here and referee in case things heat up again."

No sooner had Mr Hale left the room than Mr Thornton showed signs of waking up. Carrie dipped her fingers in the bowl of water Margaret was using for Fred and flicked them at Mr Thornton's face. He shook his head at the cold droplets hit him and opened his eyes.

"Are you ready to behave like a grown up now?" she asked.

Mr Thornton sat up, looking over to where Margaret was tending to Fred, but he didn't look as if he was about to renew the fight so Carrie went and stood by the window, her back to the rest of the room as she looked down onto the street.

"Mr Thornton," Margaret said. "I'd like you to meet my brother, Frederick."

"You have a brother?" he sounded surprised.

"Yes. Fred doesn't live in England. He is visiting because my mother is so unwell."

Mr Thornton had the good grace to look ashamed, not that Carrie could see his expression from where she stood. He looked over to her but her back and shoulders were rigid and it seemed clear that she wanted nothing to do with him. He couldn't say that he blamed her.

"I'm sorry. I have behaved shamefully and I apologise."

"No harm done," Fred said. He wasn't the type to bear grudges. "Not to me at least," he said, gesturing to where Carrie stood.

Mr Thornton looked over at her and sighed. The things he had said... he hadn't meant them, not really. He just hated the idea of her being with anyone else, it made him feel physically sick even though, in all honesty, he couldn't claim to have waited for her. She was right, he was a hypocrite.

He wondered if her stance was softening a little.

"There." Margaret declared when she had finished bathing Fred's face. "All done."

"Thank you." Fred smiled at his sister.

"And we can't send you home looking like that," Margaret told Mr Thornton.

"I'm fine, honestly."

"What would your mother think?"

"That I'm a foolish man who got into a fight."

"Please, Mr Thornton, let me at least wash away the blood."

"Honestly, Miss Hale, I am all right."

"Typical bloody man, refusing help when he needs it," Carrie said under her breath, though the others could clearly hear her. She stomped back to them and took the bowl from Margaret. "Stay!" she ordered as she sat down next to Mr Thornton on the sofa. Her fierce expression was belied by the gentleness of her touch as she dipped the cloth into the water and began to clean his abrasions. She took care not to look in to his eyes, because she was certain that she'd see contrition in them and that would surely make her want to forgive him.

She heard Fred and Margaret leave the room, gently closing the door behind them.

"Carrie," Mr Thornton said her name with such tenderness that it was almost her undoing. She bit down hard on her lower lip and focused on the cut on his cheek.

"Look at me," he pleaded.

"I can't."

He sagged slightly but didn't speak again for a few moments. Margaret rinsed the cloth out then dampened it again. She was just about to dab at his cheek when he spoke, drawing her attention to his eyes.

"Three," he said softly. "That's... what did you call it, my magic number?"

Carrie nodded, lost, as she suspected she would be, in his eyes.

"The first time it was paid for by friends of mine. I can't even remember her name. I'm not sure I ever asked. I felt so ashamed afterwards but at the time I didn't know how to say no. I didn't want to be the only virgin. The second was Sarah, a girl who regularly came into the drapers I used to work in. She was so bonny but awfully shy. I tried to draw her out every time she came in and gradually she opened up to me. When her parents found out about us they tried to put a stop to it, so we would meet up in secret. Somehow they found out and sent her off to finishing school in Switzerland. She came back a few years later, married to a London banker."

He looked very sad as he confessed that and Carrie realised that he'd had real feelings for the girl.

"Since then there's only been Anna, a woman who works at my club. She's not exactly a prostitute but she doesn't exactly play hard to get either. She picks and chooses who she wants to sleep with though. I said no for a long time, then I began to talk to her and slowly I grew to like her. It didn't seem so wrong after that."

"How often?" Carrie asked.

"Every month or so."

"And since you met me?"

"I haven't slept with her for the past three months or more and I have always used a prophylactic. My friends at school knew all about it and made sure I had something to wear even back then. I've used it ever since."

Carrie nodded with relief and went back to cleaning his cuts. She supposed she could understand him needing relief sometimes but if he hadn't used protection that would have been it. There was no way she would risk catching an STD in this backwards time.

He didn't question her further but she felt compelled to confess all the same.

"One," she admitted. "I met Mark when I was sixteen and he was twenty, he's been my only serious boyfriend. I think that's why it took me so long to end it, because... I guess I was used to him and being on my own again was scary."

"Can I ask you something?" he sounded hesitant.

"Only if you're sure you want to hear the answer."

He smiled slightly, acknowledging her point.

"How come you can fight so well?" He had noticed the scratches on her arm and had enough sense to realise that it was he who had made them before she had knocked him out.

"I was mugged," she said. "I was walking home from school when I was fourteen and these two men attacked me. They took my money, my watch, my phone, my laptop and left me with bruised ribs. I lay there waiting for someone to find me and I just decided, never again. As soon as I was healed, I started taking karate lessons. It's safe to say I was obsessed for a while but the good thing was that the instructor would spend about six weeks on technique for those who were taking an exam, then the six weeks after the exams teaching us street fighting and survival techniques. The kind of dirty fighting that isn't in any book but that saves your life. I got pretty good at one point but I don't have much time to devote to it now."

Mr Thornton brought his hands up and caught hers, stopping her from continuing her work.

"I'm sorry. And I don't just mean for you being attacked."

Carrie blinked back the tears that were stinging her eyes.

"I was an idiot," he continued. "I was hurt and jealous and angry and I took it out on the one person I shouldn't have; you. When I returned and saw you in someone else's arms I realised that I can't lose you, Carrie. It wouldn't matter to me what you did because without you, I'm nothing."

Carrie felt her lip tremble as her tears threatened to overwhelm her.

"Please say you can forgive me?"

Carrie's tears spilled over and John gently reached over with one hand and wiped them away.

"I can forgive what you said, John, but not what you did."

"What did I do?"

"In your office, you shoved me."

"I was angry, I wasn't thinking straight."

"I know, but then you attacked Fred."

"He has forgiven me, why can't you?"

"Because I won't live my life in fear. My father had a temper; we never knew how he was going to react."

"Carrie, my love, it won't happen again. You have my word."

"No, it won't... because this is goodbye, John."

She made a move to stand up and he tightened his hold on her hands, keeping her in place.

"No! No this can't be it, I won't accept that."

"If only life were that easy. Unfortunately, I am my own person and I have my own mind... and this is it, John. The way you came at me, not just physically but verbally, you were trying to wound me in whatever way you could."

"I'm sorry." He felt hot tears stinging his eyes, mirroring her own.

"I know."

"It will never happen again."

"Until the next time."

"Carrie!" He couldn't believe that this was it, that in one moment of jealousy and he had driven her away.

"No. Effective immediately, I resign my position

at Marlborough Mills and in future when you visit Mr Hale, I will not be present," Carrie said, keeping her voice as steady as she could, though tears continued to stream down her cheeks. "Now, please let go of me."

Seeing his tears was almost her undoing, but then she remembered all the times her father would plead for forgiveness and somehow, though he was not the injured party, her mother always ended up comforting him.

Finally he accepted the inevitable and released her wrists. Carrie ran from the room and fled to her bedroom, throwing herself down on the bed and sobbing her heart out.

Margaret watched as Carrie rushed passed her to their room, clearly very upset, and Margaret went back into the sitting room, fully intending to give Mr Thornton a piece of her mind. He might be a manufacturer but Carrie deserved much better than the way he was treating her and she was sure that he had it in him to be better behaved towards her friend.

What she saw as she entered stopped her diatribe cold, for Mr Thornton looked just as upset as Carrie had.

"Mr Thornton?"

He hastily wiped his eyes before turning to her but it was clear that he had been crying.

"What has happened?" she asked.

"Nothing just... Miss Preston has ended any possibility of our involvement."

"But why? I thought that she cared a great deal about you. She has been most upset since you fell out with each other."

"I think that she does care for me," he admitted. "But I have been very foolish and now I fear I have driven her away forever."

"Surely not. If she truly loves you, I do not see how she could stay away."

"Well I did not believe true love could be jealous or petty or vengeful, and yet I have found myself to be capable of all three."

"Surely not."

"If you don't mind, Miss Hale, I would really rather not discuss it any further at the moment."

"Of course. Let me make you some tea, then I shall continue cleaning your abrasions."

"That is not necessary."

"But is is, Mr Thornton, for there is something very important that we must ask of you." She turned and left, giving him a few moments to compose himself before she returned with a tray of tea. She poured two cups then she continued where Carrie had left off, bathing his face.

As she worked, she explained to Mr Thornton about Frederick. When she had finished her tale, she said a silent prayer that her father was right and that Mr Thornton could be trusted.

Despite her low opinion of him and his own confession of his character defects, Margaret found it hard to picture Mr Thornton as petty, jealous or vengeful. He just did not seem the type.

To her great relief, Mr Thornton gave his word that he would keep Fred's presence a secret, out of respect for Mr Hale if nothing else.

"Thank you, Mr Thornton," Margaret smiled, possibly the first genuine smile she had ever bestowed on him. "You are a good man."

Chapter Fourteen

Sadly Mrs Hale died on the Monday evening, adding one more woe to Carrie's burden. She tried not to get too down but at times it was hard. The Hales didn't try to cheer her, which she was glad of and although they made a pretty depressing little family, somehow they each drew strength from the other. Carrie had never been part of a family like that before; her family usually sought to attack each other in times of trouble, taking their misery out on others.

On the second day, Carrie managed to rouse her spirits enough to make the arrangements for Mrs Hale's funeral. She felt thoroughly ashamed of herself for wallowing in such self pity when the woman who had opened her home to her had just died and her family was grieving.

Thankfully, though she was not legally family, both the reverend and undertaker were very understanding and helpful. Dixon also mentioned that Mrs Hale had on occasion spoken about her funeral and she was able to give Carrie a good idea of what Mrs Hale would have wanted.

In the event though, she didn't get to attend the funeral that she had arranged. Societal norms in this time said that women couldn't go to funerals but Carrie had every intention of flouting that rule. That is until Dixon ran into Leonards, an old acquaintance from Helstone. He knew all about Frederick and the mutiny and it was decided that Fred must leave that very night.

Carrie felt bad for him that he couldn't attend his mother's funeral but at least he had gotten to say goodbye to her. As Carrie was helping him to pack his belongings, he came across a box and opened it to show Carrie the engagement ring he had bought for Dolores. She was too young to get married yet, but he had bought the ring some time ago and was just waiting until he could ask her.

The ring was quite small and the stones were only what she would have called semi-precious, yet from the way he talked about this Dolores, it was probably quite expensive. At least, he didn't seem like the kind of man to skimp on a ring when he was obviously deeply in love with this girl and that gave her an idea.

On impulse she caught the evening train to London with him. Thankfully both Margaret and Mr Hale were still too upset to question her decision very much. She and Fred booked into a respectable hotel overnight and Fred insisted on paying since Carrie did not have much money of her own. On Margaret's suggestion, Fred was to see a friend of the family and solicitor, Mr Lennox, the next day about the chances of winning a court martial and Carrie intended to get her jewellery appraised.

They dined in the Hotel's restaurant that evening and Carrie finally got the chance to really get to know Fred. Despite Mrs Hale's recent death, being somewhere new and unknown to both of them provided some distance from those sad events and allowed Carrie to see a more cheerful side of Fred than she had previously.

He told her more about Cadiz, where he lived, and his intended, Dolores, describing both his home and his beloved in such exquisite detail that it was very clear how enamoured he was of both. Carrie had lived in Spain for a time, though the land she knew was vastly different from the one he recognised, but she was able to share some of her stories with him, such as the beauty of her father's ranch and the Spanish Lipizzan horses she had been lucky enough to see while she lived there and even to ride on one occasion.

As the restaurant cleared and they had more privacy, Carrie took the opportunity to ask Fred for his account of the mutiny on his ship. It soon became clear that the glossed over incident she had read about in North and South was a pale reflection of the true cruelty of the ship's captain and Carrie was left in little doubt that the man must have been a sadist. It soon became clear that despite his easy going nature, Fred had truly risked everything, including his own life, to protect those weaker than himself and Carrie was left with a new found respect for him. So much so that she was more sorry than she should have been after such a short acquaintance, that he would be returning to Spain the following day. She vowed to keep in touch with him and if it were ever possible, to visit him there at some time.

She told him of her regret at his leaving and her desire to visit Spain as they walked back to their rooms. He stopped outside her door and leaned down to kiss her cheek.

"You will always be welcome in my home, sister," he said, smiling warmly at her.

Carrie smiled at his kind words and marvelled at how this family, that she had really known for such a short time, could have become so important to her. On impulse she hugged Fred tightly.

"Thank you, brother," she said. The language was false, for real bothers and sisters did not address each other thus, but the genuine affection behind the words made up for the awkward speech.

They bid each other goodnight before finally

retiring for the evening.

Carrie awoke early the next day, excited both to hear what Mr Lennox had to say about Fred's case and to find out the value of her jewellery, so she was surprised when Fred slipped a note under her door not ten minutes after she had awoken, saying that he would await her in the dining room so that they might breakfast together before taking care of their business. She hurried about her usual morning routine so as not to keep him waiting for too long.

By the time she joined him, Fred had already sent a message to Mr Lennox and before they left the dining hall, had received his reply. It seemed that while Mr Lennox was happy to help Fred if he could, he was unavailable until noon that day but would be pleased to see him in the afternoon. With little else to do, Fred offered to accompany Carrie to the jewellers.

Although she normally didn't place a great deal of importance on material items, Carrie's jewellery meant a lot to her because each piece had been a gift for good performance. The pendant was a reward for passing her GCSE's with A's and A stars. The earrings for passing her A-Levels. The ring for passing her grade 8 piano exam. When she wore these they were proof that she was capable of succeeding and she drew a certain strength from them.

The brooch was the only piece of jewellery that had been a gift from her mother and it was made of synthetic diamonds created using the ashes of Friday, her childhood pony. The diamonds had been mounted into a horse shaped brooch and varied in size from ¼ ct to 1ct and had a ¼ ct black diamond as an eye. Technically speaking they were exactly the same as diamonds, even down to usually having imperfections, though they often had fewer than naturally formed diamonds did.

She had decided to go to a few jewellers to have them appraised first before she asked what they would offer her to buy them.

When the first jewellers valued them, she was floored!

Since they had been gifts, she didn't know how much they cost in her time but comparatively speaking they seemed to be worth much more here.

The most expensive piece was the horse brooch, which Carrie did feel a little guilty about but she kept reminding herself that technically, right down to the molecular composition, it was made from real diamonds, albeit ones formed in a lab rather than in the earth.

The first and second shops disagreed on their valuations by almost five thousand pounds. Both also offered slightly less than they had valued them at, citing that they would need to make a profit when they sold them on.

In the third shop, a Mr Raison valued them higher than both the other shops and offered Carrie exactly what he had appraised the jewels at, saying that he would reset many of the stones from the brooch into other jewellery, which he could sell for a greater cost overall.

Since she didn't have a bank account yet and didn't want to carry cash, she arranged to return that afternoon after Fred had seen Mr Lennox and exchange the jewellery for a bankers draft.

"You're rich," Fred teased after they had collected the bankers draft.

They were heading to the railway station; Carrie's hand resting on Fred's elbow. Carrie grinned at his words, for indeed she was rich now.

"What will you spend it on?" Fred asked.

"I don't know. I suppose I should buy us a house."

"Us?" he asked.

"Your family has taken me in and treated me as one of their own, I think it only fair that I treat them the same. I wonder what houses in Milton cost?"

"I can't claim any knowledge of that," Fred said. "But I thank you for your kindness to my family. My mother said you had some very odd ideas but that she liked you very much."

"I can live with odd," she smiled. "But it is I who am thankful for them. They have been so very kind to me, and I've done little to deserve it." Carrie's mood darkened slightly. "It's just a shame that Mrs Hale won't get to share in this joy with us."

"But she will be happy that you're looking after her husband and daughter."

"I hope so." After the turmoil of the last few days, Carrie felt herself overcome with emotion.

"Oh no, you must not cry at such a happy time," Fred gently chided, handing her his handkerchief.

"I know, it is very ungrateful of me." She quickly got herself back under control and dried her eyes.

They soon arrived at the station and bought their tickets, Carrie heading north to Milton and Fred journeying south to Portsmouth.

"I know we only met recently, and in rather unhappy circumstances," Carrie said as they prepared to part company, "but I feel like I've known you forever."

She thought most people probably felt that way after meeting Fred, for he was such an affable and kind hearted person that it was hard not to like him.

"Well, you are the next best thing to a sister now," he said.

"I've never had a brother," Carrie smiled.

"Well then, the next time we meet I shall be sure to climb a few trees with you and taunt you with some captured insects so that you have a true appreciation of what having a brother feels like."

"*That* I think I'll pass on," Carrie laughed, then hugged him tightly. "Now, you take care on your journey home. And please write if Mr Lennox has any news, good or bad."

"I will. You look after yourself too, won't you?"

"I will," she assured him. "Say hello to Dolores for me."

As she rode back to Milton, Carrie felt lighter than she had for some time. She had means now. She could never have dreamed how much her jewellery would be worth here, especially since so few women wore diamonds, she had assumed they were unpopular. How wrong she had been.

The first thing she would do was buy a house for them all. Then a piano. She could even give lessons on it if she wanted to.

Then perhaps she could buy more houses to rent out? Yes, that would be a good long term investment and provide them with a steady, regular income.

Her mind immediately went to Mr Thornton as the best person to ask for advice but she couldn't ask him any longer. That thought dampened her spirits somewhat and try as she may, she was unable to revive them again.

Chapter Fifteen

The house Carrie bought was in a nicer area of Milton; a little further away from the mills and so also slightly less smoky. They kept most of the same furniture since it had a history with the family, though Carrie did buy new furnishings for the dining room and the front parlour, in other words the public rooms. The furniture she chose was nice but not overly expensive.

She had noticed that many homes in Milton, Mr Thornton's included, were very over-done, almost as though families needed to show their wealth off if they had it. The decoration was too ornate, the light fixtures too grand and the furniture usually large, dark and imposing. Most homes were also full of ornaments and many reflective surfaces. She found it all too stuffy, cluttered and cold for her tastes and so thanks to its simplicity and homey ambiance, this house still felt much more like the Hale's home in Crampton than Mr Thornton's fine house.

Her only luxury was in purchasing a Broadwood grand piano, which took pride of place in the front parlour (or the fancy sitting room, as Carrie thought of it).

Mr Hale had a study where he could teach his students and Miss Hale could use the rear parlour (the less fancy sitting room or family room, as Carrie called it) while Carrie could teach piano in the front parlour.

They hired a third full time servant to help Dixon and a cook who preferred to live out, but the extra help meant that Dixon was able to resume her original role as lady's maid, though she insisted on also keeping the position of housekeeper so that the house might be run to her own exacting standards. Carrie didn't mind as long as Dixon didn't have to work as hard, for she was starting to look rather tired at times.

There was a spare room beside the kitchen, which was turned into a sitting room for Dixon and shared by cook while she was on duty. Since the attic had four bedrooms when only three were needed, the other two servants shared the fourth room and made it into their sitting room.

Mr Hale informed some of his students and their families that Carrie was about to start giving piano lessons and he advised her on what she could charge. Sadly it was only a fraction of what Mr Hale got for his teaching, but this wasn't supposed to be her main form of income anyway. That's why she was buying more properties, two mid-sized ones, like the one in Crampton that could be more easily rented than larger properties could and some commercial properties, since the rents for such premises were generally higher. She wasn't foolish though and still kept some some in the bank for a rainy day. She hoped that the rental incomes combined with her and Mr Hale's lessons would cover their living expenses and perhaps allow her to put a little more into the bank every month.

Of course news of her new found wealth had spread like wildfire, though most reports were highly inflated, and she found herself inundated with new friends and acquaintances. She wasn't particularly inclined to make friends with these people but she knew well enough not to alienate them, especially when she was trying to build her teaching business. One thing her mother had taught her was the necessity of forging relationships. As such she accepted most of their dinner invitations, if only for appearance's sake.

As autumn finally gave way to winter, Carrie was surprised to learn from Mr Hale that Christmas was a relatively new celebration. Christmas had always been on the 25th of December, of course, but the pomp and circumstance surrounding the day owed its recent revival to Prince Albert popularising some of his German traditions, such as decorating Christmas trees, and to Charles Dickens book, A Christmas Carol.

Carrie threw herself into decorating the house, making wreathes, buying ornaments for the tree and decorating the mantelpiece with pine tree branches, holly and mistletoe berries. The tree was placed in the family room where they could all enjoy it in the evenings. When Mr Hale heard that Mr Southard's parents were travelling and that his elder brother was already married with his own family, he extended an invitation to spend Christmas day with them and Mr Southard accepted.

Dixon ordered the turkey, though she was puzzled by Carrie's insistence of serving the expensive bird, and the family exchanged small presents on Christmas Eve. Carrie had put a limit on the cost of presents so that no one bought anything too expensive; she was worried that the Hales would feel that they owed her, when the truth was she still felt she owed them for taking her in. Dixon refused to join them as they exchanged gifts, which Margaret informed Carrie had always been her way, so they left her presents under the servants' tree in the room next to the kitchen.

Margaret gave Carrie a set of hand-made roses as hair ornaments. Seeing how much Carrie had liked the pink one she had made for Mrs Thornton's dinner party, Margaret had made a variety of similar decorations in various colours.

Mr Hale had bought her a collection of Jane Austin books. Though all seemed second hand, Carrie didn't care for she enjoyed Austin almost as much as she used to enjoy Gaskell.

In turn Carrie bought Margaret a new pair of kid gloves similar to ones she had once admired on Mr Slickson's wife and Mr Hale received a set of personalised stationary and a new quill and selection of nibs for his correspondence. Indeed it seemed to Carrie that rarely a day passed when he did not have some old friend or acquaintance to reply to.

For Dixon, Carrie purchased a set of glass bottles and pots of various sizes that were housed in a leather case, for her to store the lotions and potions that she made for the young women. Dixon was surprised by the gift but very pleased.

Mr Thornton had heard of Carrie's good fortune, for surely no one in Milton hadn't, but unlike them he got his information direct from her banker, Mr Latimer, who coincidentally happened to be his banker also.

He was pleased to hear that she was making solid investments and not spending wildly because although he couldn't have her, all he really wanted was for her to be happy and secure.

Though he longed to see her again, even if only for a moment, she had kept to her word and was never around when he went to see Mr Hale. Every time he journeyed through the town his eyes roamed around him, seeking her out, though so far he had not been successful.

That was about to change though, for he had been invited to the Waverley's annual Christmas dinner party this evening and after casually enquiring, had been informed that the Hales and Miss Preston would be attending also.

Carrie might have said that he felt as nervous as a virgin on prom night but though it was true, such crude though evocative language was beyond him. He wondered if she would rescind her acceptance if she knew he was coming and for that reason he hadn't confirmed his own attendance until the last acceptable moment.

As he approached the Waverley's house he began to feel slightly sick but he forced himself to ignore the sensation; then as he stepped into the parlour his breath literally caught in his throat, for there she was in all her glory and he found that his memory of her had been sadly lacking when compared to the reality.

She laughed at something her companion said and his heart sank, for he knew when she was being polite and when she was genuinely enjoying someone's company and this time it was the latter. To make things even worse, he even respected her companion, the M.P. Bernard Southard.

"Thornton, my dear fellow, how are you?"

And with those words the spell was broken. Carrie turned to him, looking almost frightened. Had he really scared her so? He didn't think so but the reality was unavoidable. It didn't take her long to smooth her features into perfect serenity again and turn away. Thornton turned his attention to Mr Waverley, who had uttered the earlier greeting.

He couldn't help but notice how many men surrounded Carrie all evening and he was forced to remember his dinner party, when hardly anyone had spoken to her. He supposed her fortune made her a much more attractive proposition now.

Thankfully every time he looked over she seemed

as if she was trying to stifle her boredom and Mr Southard had now moved on and was speaking with Miss Hale, whom he seemed most taken with. Those facts combined to give him hope that at least he would not lose Carrie to anyone present this evening.

It was a most agreeable surprise to find that when dinner was called, he had been seated next to her; a most delightful place to be, though it had not been his scheme.

"Mr Thornton." She flashed him a sickly sweet smile. "How lovely it is to see you again." Each word dripped with sarcasm.

"And you," he smiled warmly, not rising to the bait.

"I suppose this is your idea?"

"Why would Mrs Waverley consult me over her seating plan?"

Carrie was forced to agree that she wouldn't, not that she would admit it.

They ignored each other for the rest of the first course, only talking with others at the table until the plates were cleared.

"You look lovely this evening," Mr Thornton said quietly.

Caught off guard, Carrie could only reply. "Thank you."

"How are you?" he asked.

"I'm fine."

He smiled and turned away again, content with a polite, if somewhat simple, exchange for now.

The main course and dessert were served without any further conversation between them but Carrie was on tenterhooks the whole time, wondering what he was going to do next but in the end it was their hostess who put Carrie on the spot, not

Mr Thornton.

"I say, Mr Thornton, have you heard Miss Preston play yet?" Mrs Waverley asked from where she sat at the end of the table.

Mr Thornton knew about her giving piano lessons, obviously, for it was hard not to know the details of her life these days. Indeed since coming into her fortune, Miss Preston had been the topic of conversation at many dining tables throughout Milton.

"I regret to say that I have not had that pleasure yet," he told Mrs Waverly.

"Oh, you simply must, she is a beautiful pianist, isn't she?"

There was a general consensus of 'yes' from the table, even from those who had never heard her and Carrie blushed.

"And she has done wonders for Emily's playing; why she has come on in leaps and bounds since Miss Preston began teaching her. Perhaps we can convince Miss Preston to grace us with a tune after dessert."

"But the gentlemen will remain at the table, surely," Carrie smiled sweetly, though it was a little tight after having been thrust into the spotlight like this.

"Then let them stay. I'm sure once they hear your playing, they will be drawn through to hear you better anyway."

"We'll see," Carrie smiled, hoping that was the end of it.

After dessert the ladies retired to the drawing room while the men stayed at the table, drinking brandy and smoking cigars. Nothing more was said about Carrie playing and she breathed a sigh of relief until the gentlemen joined them.

"Now Miss Preston, I hope you have not forgotten your promise," Mrs Waverley called from across the room.

Carrie had promised no such thing but she could hardly embarrass her hostess by causing a scene. Besides, the Waverley's had been very good about recommending her to other local families.

"Of course not." She smiled as graciously as she could and made her way over to the grand piano in the corner of the room. She didn't have any music with her, obviously, so she opted to play Memory from Cats since she knew it by heart.

She could feel his eyes on her as she played and though she didn't have any music to focus on, she kept her eyes downcast, looking at her hands so that she didn't have to look at him.

When she finished everyone clapped and she wondered what they would think if they could actually see the musical that song came from; the cast dressed in cat costumes and makeup!

Mrs Waverley called for a second song and though Carrie protested she was pushed into it. She played Exogenesis Symphony by Muse.

When she was done they applauded politely again and she stood up to make it clear that she was finished. Thankfully Mrs Waverely didn't press her any further.

However, in not looking at the people around her while she played, she had made a fatal mistake because Mr Thornton was suddenly in front of her.

"That was exquisite," he told her, his voice full of warmth and love.

Carrie swallowed and wondered where her glass of wine had gone.

"Thank you," she kept her head bowed because she knew that if she looked at him, it would be her undoing.

"Perhaps you might like to teach Fanny. She has been having lessons for years but has never really mastered the instrument."

"I believe I am full at the moment, but perhaps after the New Year."

"Do I really frighten you that much?"

Carrie looked up, shocked by such a statement. Then she remembered why she had refused him. He might be sweetness and light now but she had seen another side of him.

Mr Thornton noticed the hesitation in her eyes and how her resolve suddenly hardened once again and he began to wonder; was she really afraid of him or was that an excuse?

His behaviour had been inexcusable that day but she didn't seem afraid of him. Mr Southard and Margaret interrupted them then and Mr Thornton drifted off to speak to someone else, realising that he must not press her too hard too quickly.

As he lay in bed that night, his mind kept drifting back over her actions and reactions earlier that evening and while he was sure he had seen genuine fear in her eyes, he didn't think that she was frightened of him, per se. He began to ponder what kind of threat he actually posed to her because he was certain, with all her karate skills, that there was very little that frightened Miss Preston.

Then he remembered the first time he met her. He had thought her shy back then, noting the blush on her cheeks as she thanked him for his help in getting the wallpapers changed.

He had put her reticence down to her not knowing the customs here in the north and later, after he discovered where she was really from, being unfamiliar with 19th century customs at all.

Now though he saw that she actually was shy; she was just rather practised at overcoming it.

He had everything backwards, he realised. Everything frightened the girl and she just showed incredible bravery in fighting back.

He began to realise that his judgement of her was flawed and had always been flawed.

When she had spoken about being attacked when she was 14, she had said how helpless she felt as she lay waiting for help. Of course she had felt powerless, he had reasoned, having been overcome by two men but perhaps it was her disposition to feel powerless, perhaps that is how she had been raised.

He remembered Fanny attacking her behaviour for fighting and how initially Carrie had not defended herself; only Fanny's continued taunts had finally goaded her enough to defend her actions.

He remembered her saying that her father had a temper and that she would never live her life in fear again. Had he been violent? And yet she still carried a photograph of him in her purse and had more on her laptop. Clearly she still loved him.

He groaned and wiped a hand over his face, as though washing without water. Of course!

She had loved her father and he had betrayed her trust in him and broken her heart, possibly because he was violent but certainly because he had a temper.

Mr Thornton could see now that the power he had to wound her far exceeded any black eye, for he had the power to break her heart again.

He wouldn't, of course, he had just been half crazed that day. Who wouldn't be after hearing such an outlandish tale and finding out that their perfect vision of a woman was impure? It wasn't in his nature to react violently, he was a calm and rational man usually. He had examined his behaviour closely since she had sent him away and truly that had been an aberration.

Now the question became, how could he prove that to her?

Chapter Sixteen

When news of Mr Watson's speculation reached Carrie, she found herself with something of a quandary. She knew that Mr Thornton would not invest in such a risky venture and she also knew from the book that it was his only hope for saving the mill. Though he was trying his best to keep the business afloat, the strike had hit him hard, both in lost revenue and fines on late orders.

Of course in the book, that was the reason that he and Margaret finally admitted their love for each other, when she was able to ride to his rescue. Here though even if they had been in love, that was impossible, for Mr Hale was still alive and Mr Bell had not made Margaret his heir, so as such Margaret had no money to invest in the mill.

In the book she knew the speculation succeeded but here, since so many things had changed, there was no saying that the result of this speculation might not be different also. Should she try to convince Mr Thornton to invest, or should she leave well enough alone? It took her many sleepless nights wrestling with the possibilities before she finally came to a decision.

Though he thought about it for many days, Mr Thornton finally decided against making any grand plans to win Carrie back because he knew her well enough to realise that schemes wouldn't work. The only way she would learn to trust him was if she spent time with him again so that he could show her that he really was trustworthy.

Of course, that was the easy part. The hard part was convincing her to spend time with him at all!

Instead he had decided to put a recent idea into action.

For a few months now, Carrie's words, 'be the change you want to see' had been on his mind and he had come up with a somewhat hare-brained scheme. He had thought it through from many angles and found it to be a very flawed plan indeed, nevertheless it kept plaguing him and finally he had decided to act.

As he made his way through Milton's slums, the conditions came as something of a shock to him. They shouldn't of course, for he had been here before and yet somehow time always seemed to dim the horror until he was directly confronted with it again.

He walked up to former union leader, Nicholas Higgins's front door and knocked swiftly. Higgins looked surprised to see a Milton master at his door, probably more so since he had never worked for Thornton, but nevertheless he stepped back and invited him in.

Mr Thornton smiled slightly for though they were considered enemies, northern hospitality still prevailed.

Although the home was small, he had done his best to keep it clean and homely. The stone floor looked to have been scrubbed to within an inch of its life and although the kitchen table, which took up most of the room downstairs, had clearly seen better days, Mr Thornton thought that he'd be happy to eat his dinner off it. A rather remarkable feat considering that there were eight young children in the house and one teenager.

"Are they all yours?" Mr Thornton asked.

"Not the younger ones but they're mine now," Higgins explained. "A neighbour of ours were driven mad by the strike. He killed himself."

"And his wife?"

"Soon followed her husband." It was clear by his clipped tone that it wasn't a subject he wanted to go into in any great detail. "I take it Miss Preston sent you?"

"Miss Preston? Why would she-?"

"I've been looking for work and for obvious reasons, not having an easy time of it. She suggested I try you, said you were an honourable man and would hear me out."

"Did she?" Mr Thornton wasn't sure what to make of that. "You are still friendly with the Hales then?"

"Aye. They may have a grand 'ouse now but they still welcome those they were friendly with afore."

"I would expect nothing less."

"So," Nicholas gestured to the table, meaning for Mr Thornton to take a seat. "If Miss Preston didn't send you here, I must say I'm puzzled by your visit."

"Probably no more than I am by making it," Mr Thornton answered as he sat down.

Although no one had asked her, the oldest child, the teenager, had begun making tea and now handed them both a mug and placed a pot between them.

"I'm sorry, we've no milk or sugar," the girl said, blushing at the thought of speaking directly to a mill master.

"Black is fine," he assured her, wanting to spare her embarrassment. "Thank you."

"So, what brings you here?" Higgins asked as he served the tea.

"I have questioned myself constantly on why it is I wish to speak with you but I can find no reasonable answers, other than the fact that the current working conditions, the animosity between workers and masters cannot continue."

"So you've come here to make peace?" Nicholas managed to sound both surprised and affronted. "Forgive me but I thought you masters had already got your way."

"The workers have returned, that is true, but the bad feeling remains."

"And how do you propose to end it?" Nicholas asked.

"I have no firm answers for you," Mr Thornton answered honestly. "I have a few ideas but I was hoping that between us we might be able to come up with some kind of workable plan."

"All the while you masters keep cutting pay and expecting us to lump it, there will never be peace between us. Prices rise almost daily and even reasonable sized families have trouble managing. Those with large families, widows and widowers and those with ill relatives would starve were it not for the kindness of their neighbours, who can ill afford charity themselves."

"I did not come here for a sermon," Mr Thornton said, irritated by his harsh words, though he tried very hard not to sound angry. "You make it sound like we enjoy cutting wages."

"Don't you? We don't see you taking a pay cut, you still keep your fancy houses and your fancy clothes and your-"

"You shouldn't judge a book by its cover," Mr Thornton snapped. "While it is true that some masters do live in luxury others, such as myself, merely have to keep up appearances. My fine clothes are none younger than three years old and have been expertly darned many times by my mother. The only indulgence I have had since the market hit hard times has been the money I spend on my sister, though thankfully she will soon be someone else's responsibility."

Higgins was inclined to snort and roll his eyes but something in Mr Thornton's tone made him believe that the man spoke the truth.

"If times really are that hard, why retain the maids in your home?"

"I have considered firing some but like the workers in the mill, they have families to feed also. Which one should I fire? Jane, whose new husband drinks away most of her wages? Or Sarah, who lives with her widowed mother and supports her brothers and sisters. Or Cook perhaps, whose husband still cannot find employment after the strike and whose children are all too young to work."

"Aye," Higgins conceded. "I see your point."

"And I see yours," Mr Thornton agreed. "Believe me, I take no pride in my hands having to live somewhere like this."

"So what's to do?" Higgins asked.

"That's why I'm here," Mr Thornton said. "I'm hoping that between us we can find some solutions; ways to ease troubles for both workers and masters."

"Masters? You mean the others have agreed to this meeting?"

"No," Mr Thornton gave a wry smile. "But I am hoping that if we are successful, some of the others might follow my lead."

Higgins nodded and considered Thornton for a while before speaking again.

"Right. Well the way I see it, the biggest problem facing people is food. The prices get higher whilst the wages get lower."

"Well the best way to get a good deal on anything is to buy it wholesale," Mr Thornton quickly answered. "Cooking for twenty is much cheaper than for one at a time."

So the first practical step they decided upon was to try and open a canteen in the factory, so that food could be purchased wholesale and bought by the workers for a fraction of the cost, ensuring that all the hands had at least one good meal a day. Higgins had agreed to work out the costings and as they talked, Mr Thornton was somewhat surprised to realise what a keen mind Higgins had. He would have made a fair businessman if he'd had the education or opportunity.

Higgins also agreed to work at Marlborough Mill, on the condition that he would give Mr Thornton fair warning if he found anything wrong and on the understanding that he would be a kind of go-between for the master and the hands.

Although the workers were initially distrustful of the scheme, a week later the canteen opened and the workers quickly began to realise the bargain price of the meals on offer. Higgins daughter, Mary, prepared the food, usually something plentiful and simple like stew or casserole, and she baked fresh bread every morning. Before the week was out some workers had begun asking if they might buy more than one meal and take the food home with them. Neither Mr Thornton nor Higgins could see any problem with that and by the third week, Mary found herself the boss of the kitchen, since she now had two young girls helping her each day.

The next issue that Higgins wanted to address was sick pay and as they shared lunch in the canteen one day, Higgins outlined his plan for the master. Mr Thornton was initially distrustful, assuming that

Higgins wanted him to pay workers who couldn't work, but Higgins had already thought this through and had a very different scheme in mind.

"Those who are willing will pay a small amount into a sick fund every week. Those who are taken ill and who have paid into the fund can then receive a wage for up to twelve days out of every two years. In the event of a death, the widows could claim the sick pay for twelve weeks to help tide them over until sommat else can be worked out."

"And what if they have not taken their sick days?" Mr Thornton asked, "Is there not a danger that people will abuse it and take time off when they are not really ill?"

"The sick wage would have to be lower than the normal wage so not many would, but if anyone does abuse the system, they're out," Higgins explained.

"And who would administer this?"

"Well me to start, with help from a couple of t'lads."

"Well, if it's my permission you're after, you have it."

"Thank you, Master, but as nice as that is we do need your help."

"If you are organising this amongst yourselves, I hardly see what use I could be. Indeed some workers would likely distrust the scheme if I were directly involved."

"You're not wrong on that score, Master." Higgins flashed him a wry smile. "The thing is we need a bank account. As much faith as I have in my fellow man, there's very few of us that is above temptation under the right circumstances."

"And you don't think the bank would look very favourably on you wanting to open an account?"

"Exactly. Some liberal-thinking gentlemen help

180

the unions open their accounts and I was hoping you'd do the same for us."

Mr Thornton nodded, stood up and held his hand out to Higgins.

"I will speak with Mr Latimer tomorrow. I am sure he will be amenable."

"Thank you, Master." Higgins shook his hand and then returned to work.

Carrie heard all about Mr Thornton's schemes from Higgins when he came to see Mr Hale. He wasn't as frequent a visitor any more because he now had work again, but he tried to stop in on a Sunday if he could.

Carrie had been pleased as punch to hear that not only had John employed Higgins under his own steam but that he also seemed to be trying to change the cotton industry and take better care of his workers.

Bernard Southard cared a lot about the plight of the working classes and, using his position as an M.P. he was doing his best to ease their plight. When he came to share tea with the family, he took a great deal of interest in what Mr Hale told him about the schemes going on at Marlborough Mills. Though he admitted that he couldn't legislate for such schemes, he was interested in ways he might be able to encourage other employers to adopt similar arrangements.

"Perhaps you could offer a lower tax rate to those who implement similar systems," Margaret suggested to him.

"A wonderful idea," he smiled warmly at her. "But I will have my work cut out for me in persuading others that reducing taxes is a good idea, but perhaps I might be able to do something along those lines. Perhaps I could make money used for such ventures tax deductible, but even that will be difficult."

Mr Southard seemed to take a great deal of pleasure in talking with Margaret and always listened patiently to her suggestions, however naive they might be. Ever since he had met the Hales and Miss Preston at Mrs Thornton's dinner party, he had been a regular visitor at the house but over the past few months his visits had started to become almost weekly.

Today he revealed that his intention in coming was to ask them to an opera that was being performed in his home town of Lampton the following evening. He used the pretext of having been let down and having tickets to spare but as Carrie observed him, she thought that this was an excuse to save his blushes should they refuse, and he simply wanted to spend more time with Margaret. He needn't have worried, for Margaret seemed just as taken with him as he was with her.

Carrie was about to decline so that he might be able to spend some time alone with Margaret, as she was sure he wanted but when Mr Hale accepted, she agreed to go also in the hopes that she could divert Mr Hale at times and allow the couple some time together.

The opera was the Barber of Seville. Carrie knew only a little about it since though she loved music, she claimed no great knowledge of opera. She made sure to take Mr Hale's arm when they arrived at the theatre so that Mr Southard could escort Margaret inside and then she proceeded to ask Mr Hale many questions about the opera so as to keep him occupied.

Mr Hale happily explained the plot to her while

they had drinks before the performance started, which allowed Margaret and Mr Southard a chance to talk.

After the play Mr Southard took them to a local hotel for dinner and Carrie suggested that they walk there since it wasn't far. She made sure to keep Mr Hale engaged in conversation while they walked so that he didn't notice how far behind Margaret and Mr Southard were falling, though they always remained in sight.

By the time they took a carriage home at the end of the evening, Margaret looked flushed with pleasure and though she envied Margaret her happiness, Carrie was pleased for her.

Unlike Mr Thornton, Mr Southard was a gentleman, the son of a Duke and educated at Eton. His elder brother was to inherit the title and family estate, so Bernard had chosen politics as his vocation in life. He was perfect for Margaret in that he was gentry, wealthy and had a social conscience. Carrie could hardly have written a more sublime match for her, and she supposed that was why Elizabeth Gaskell hadn't written Mr Southard as Margaret's mate, for there was no dramatic tension in perfection.

While Mr Hale dozed in the carriage, Margaret and Carrie softly discussed the evening, whispering to each other like a pair of schoolgirls. It seemed that the psychic had been correct and Margaret would indeed find happiness with a politician.

"I must write to Mr Southard tomorrow and thank him for such a pleasant evening." Mr Hale said as they entered the house. "Why I don't remember the last time I had such a delightful evening. And the play was enchanting, don't you agree?"

"Yes, Papa," Margaret smiled.

"Mr Southard is such a congenial fellow," Mr Hale continued.

"Isn't he?" Carrie asked rhetorically, flashing a sly smile at Margaret behind Mr Hales back and causing the other girl to blush.

"Indeed." Mr Hale turned to them once he had hung up his hat and coat. "Well, it is rather late so I think I shall retire to bed. Goodnight." He leaned down so both girls could kiss his cheek in turn.

"Goodnight, Father," Margaret said after she had kissed him.

"Sleep well," Carrie said.

Though they were far too excited to sleep, the girls headed to bed as well, though Carrie stayed in Margaret's bedroom as they talked into the wee small hours, gossiping about Mr Southard.

Carrie usually got up in her own time in the mornings so it was something of a surprise when Carrie awoke to find Dixon gently shaking her shoulder, though she assumed that she must have fallen asleep in Margaret's bed and Dixon was waking her to return to her own room. Either that or she had overslept since they were awake until late the night before.

"Dixon?" she asked, as she rubbed her eyes. She realised that she had made it back to her own room before falling asleep last night. "What time is it?"

"Still early, Miss, not yet seven, Miss," Dixon said.

Carrie's heart sank as she was finally awake enough to take in Dixon's grief stricken countenance.

Chapter Seventeen

Carrie listened as Dixon hurriedly and quietly explained why she was here, though Carrie thought that she already had a good idea what brought the servant into their room at this ungodly hour of the morning.

"See I always bring Mr Hale some warm water at this time since he is such an early riser but this morning he was still sound asleep."

"Oh no," she sighed.

"I tried to wake him but he won't wake, Miss. He just lies there, looking to the whole world as if he's sound asleep."

Carrie swiftly got out of bed and as quietly as they could, they made their way along the hallway to Mr Hale's bedroom. While Mr Hale did indeed look peaceful, his face was so pale that Carrie didn't think for a moment that he was merely sleeping. She approached the bed and touched her fingers to his neck. Not only was there no pulse, he was cool to the touch, meaning that he had been dead for some time.

"I don't think he suffered," Carrie told Dixon, who hovered in the doorway, her handkerchief clutched in her hands. "Whatever happened, it was swift and wasn't enough to waken him."

Dixon nodded. "Should I wake Miss Margaret?" Dixon asked.

"No," Carrie said, moving to join Dixon by the door. "We were up late last night, gossiping, so she needs her rest, and this might be the last true rest she gets for a while."

Dixon nodded her agreement.

"Let's you and I go downstairs and have a

cup of tea."

All the servants were fond of Mr Hale and both the girls took it hard. Cook hadn't come for the day yet but she hadn't known Mr Hale very well so she would probably take the news of his death the easiest of all.

Carrie and Dixon listened as the younger servants shared stories of Mr Hale, how kind he had been to them, or perhaps when he had been a little absent minded, or had made them laugh. He was such an easy going gentleman and far different to any men the servants had known before. Men in the north tended to be hard and driven, while Mr Hale always seemed relaxed and often had a slightly scatterbrained air about him.

They could hear when Margaret awoke, since her bedroom was above the kitchen and her faint footfalls could be heard above them. Carrie made to stand up but Dixon placed a hand on her arm.

"I've known her the longest, Miss. It should be me."

Since Dixon had awoken her, Carrie had assumed that she didn't want to tell Margaret the news herself, but she was right, she had known Margaret since she was a child and the news might be easier coming from Dixon.

"If you're sure," Carrie said.

"I am."

When she had gone, Carrie turned to the other two servants.

"I wonder if one of you would be so good as to fetch Doctor Donaldson for us, please? Tell him there is no rush. Your usual duties are suspended for the moment so please just do your best to see to Miss Margaret's needs and assist Cook with any help she might require. In fact I'm sure only one of you need be here at a time if you would like to take this opportunity to visit your families, that's fine. Your wages won't be docked."

"Thank you, Miss." they answered in unison.

They were both good girls who had an excellent work ethic and who could be trusted, so Carrie had no qualms about them abusing her charity. Besides, the house was in mourning, somehow dusting the crystal and beating the rugs just seemed far too pedestrian to be done at a time like this.

Carrie left them to it, wanting to see how Margaret was fairing. She found her in Dixon's arms, the maid softly crooning to her as she held Margaret in her arms.

Not wanting to intrude, Carrie went to her room and cried in private for a few moments before dressing for the day and heading downstairs to await Dr Donaldson. The next few weeks were going to be hard on all of them, so Carrie had to stay strong.

Bad news always travels fast and so it was with a heavy heart that Higgins, having heard the news himself from one of the cart drivers, approached Mr Thornton at eleven that morning.

"Mr Hale? Dead?" Mr Thornton asked, seemingly unable to process the news.

"Aye. Went in his sleep apparently."

"What of Miss Hale and Miss Preston?"

"Miss Hale's in a state by all accounts though Miss Preston seems composed."

'But she isn't,' Mr Thornton thought. *'She's being strong because she has to be for Margaret's sake, but who is there for her when she needs someone to lean on?'*

"Master?"

"Sorry, what did you say?"

"I said Mary and I were thinking of going round this evening, if you'd like to come with us."

"I fear I would not be welcome at such a time. Miss Hale is no great friend and Miss Preston's feelings towards me are less than cordial. I fear that seeing me would offer them no comfort and might even make them feel worse."

"Nonsense," Higgins said. "No one cares for petty grievances at times like these. They'll be glad to see you. Both of 'em."

"Maybe," John nodded, accepting his reasoning. "Perhaps I'll go round and see them this afternoon, see if there's anything I can do."

Higgins shrugged, not unduly bothered that Mr Thornton hadn't taken him up on his offer.

"Well, I just thought you should know," Higgins said. "I'd best get on."

"Right," Mr Thornton acknowledged, though it seemed clear that his mind was elsewhere. He walked back across the courtyard to the office and sat behind his desk, steepling his hands under his chin as he thought.

He went back and forth, mulling over various ideas, rejecting them only to rethink, dust them off and consider them again.

Finally he reached a decision and, dipping his nib into his ink well, he began composing a letter.

"Miss Preston!"

Carrie turned at the sound of her name and felt her heart skip a beat as she saw Mr Thornton jogging across the road to catch up with her.

"Miss Preston, how are you?" he asked as he finally stopped in front of her.

"Fine, thank you. I'm keeping busy which

is helping."

"Where are you off to?" he asked, wondering where she was heading. She was dressed from head to toe in black which made her already pale complexion look positively translucent and highlighted the dark circles under her eyes.

"The funeral home," she answered, as though it was obvious.

"Mr Hale only died this morning?"

"Yes, I know, but it has to be done at sometime and right now I feel rather numb so it's probably best to make the arrangements before I turn into a basket case."

"Then allow me to accompany you."

"There's really no need," she insisted.

"I think there is. I think that Mr Hale would be shocked and appalled at my behaviour if I let a young, grieving woman attend a funeral home on her own."

Carrie should have said no, but right now she didn't have the strength, so she took his elbow and allowed him to escort her.

"How is Miss Hale handling the news?" he asked.

"Well, under the circumstances. I believe she is numb."

"Will you write to her brother?" he asked.

"I have been wondering about that. I know he would rush home and I'm sure he would be a great comfort to Margaret but I am equally sure that if he should be caught, that would be a calamity. I'm not sure Margaret could recover if Fred were to be hanged. She would have lost her entire family within a year."

"I think perhaps you are right," he said. "It might please you to know that I have written to Mr Hale's old friend, Mr Bell. He has often spoken to me about the Hales with much warmth and he was the one who put Mr Hale in touch with me in the first place. I'm sure he will hurry to be with Margaret at this difficult time.

"Oh, that would be marvellous." she smiled up at him looking relieved and grateful. "Thank you, Mr Thornton, that was very thoughtful of you."

"Will you not call me John?" he asked.

"Thank you, John."

"Is there anything I can do for you?" he asked.

"I'm fine, honestly. Sending for someone to comfort Margaret was more than enough."

"But who is to comfort you?" he asked, stopping and turning to face her.

"I need no comfort, Mr Thornton. Really, I have hardly known Mr Hale any time at all. Dixon has more right to be upset than I."

"But you cared for him, I know you did, and you have every right to grieve for him; just as much right as Margaret and Dixon."

She began to cry, her tears silently falling over her cheeks. Mr Thornton withdrew his handkerchief and gently wiped them away for her.

"You are too kind, John," she said, struggling to get her emotions back in check. She didn't like to look weak in front of him.

Mr Thornton smiled softly at her.

"It's nothing more than you deserve," he assured her. Knowing that she was uncomfortable, he handed her his handkerchief and turned in the direction they had been heading. She took his elbow again and they continued walking in silence until they reached the funeral parlour.

Once inside, the funeral director, Mr Helman, was most solicitous and offered Margaret all the time she needed to make a decision. Realising that she should confirm things with Margaret, or at the very least Dixon, before she committed to anything, she thanked him for his time and assured him that she would return as soon as she knew what the family wanted.

Having helped her to arrange Mrs Hale's funeral, Mr Helman knew she was a woman of her word and was quite content that she would get back to him in a reasonable length of time.

"I suppose you and Miss Hale will return to London now?" Mr Helman asked. Even though he was old enough to be their grandfather, he was still sorry to see two beautiful young women leave Milton. There was not enough beauty in this northern mill town and anything, or anyone, who helped brighten it up a little would be missed.

"I hadn't thought," Carrie confessed. "But yes, I suppose."

"You will be sorely missed, the both of you," Mr Helman said, clasping her hand in both of his. "And once again, I'm sorry for your loss."

"Thank you."

Margaret turned to leave and Mr Thornton accompanied her. He was unable to speak for a long while as he contemplated her leaving Milton. It hadn't even occurred to him that she might leave and if she did... Well, then his chance of ever being with her was well and truly over.

Carrie hadn't considered returning to London, or she supposed she and Margaret could now go and live in Spain with Fred. That thought might cheer Margaret up, she thought. She also wondered if it might not be easier to live without Mr Thornton if she were living somewhere else, without the daily reminders and mentions of his name. Would that make it easier to forget him?

She looked over at him. His features were stern as he frowned and she found herself reaching out to take his elbow again. He looked down at her hand and his his frown melted away.

"Do you really dislike this town so very much?" He finally managed to ask her.

"No," she assured him. "But Margaret and I are two single women now; it would be very unseemly for us to live alone together."

"Nonsense," he assured her. "Widows often live alone, and you aren't alone, you have three servants living with you. There is nothing unseemly about that. Besides, I thought you enjoyed flouting convention."

"I wouldn't say I enjoy it," she answered. "But it is necessary sometimes. Still, I wouldn't like to live up here on my own."

"Then stay with us, we have more than enough room, especially now that Fanny has married."

"Thank you, but I wouldn't want to be a burden."

"You could never be a burden," he assured her.

"But Margaret is the closest thing I have to family and if she will have me, I would like to stay with her."

Mr Thornton stopped and nodded curtly.

"Message received and understood, Miss Preston," he said, carefully removing her hand from his elbow. "You are nearly home now so I think it best if I take my leave. Good day, Miss Preston, please extend my regards to Miss Hale."

Before Carrie had time to process his words, he was already striding away. What had she said that was so awful?

She reviewed the conversation and realised that she had rejected him once again. Somehow he had found the courage to offer for her again, though in a very different way, and once again she had turned him down. No wonder he was upset.

Carrie trudged back to her home and with a leaden heart, went to join Margaret in the back parlour. Somehow in one day she had lost the closest thing she had to a father and any chance she might have had for marriage.

For despite her harsh words, there was still a tiny part of her that craved Mr Thornton's attentions and wanted him to find his way back to her. Somehow though, and without even meaning to, she had offended him again and judging by how hurt he had looked, he might never forgive her.

She tried to remember exactly why she had sent him away but in her grief she was unable to recall anything but the longing she felt for his presence and the comfort it gave her.

Chapter Eighteen

Mr Bell arrived the next day, having caught the next train from Oxford as soon as he received Mr Thornton's letter.

He was a great comfort to Margaret, and the two of them talked for hours about Mr Hale, his eccentricities and their memories of him. Carrie listened to these conversations but she didn't often partake.

Mr Bell helped Carrie with the funeral arrangements and generally helped everyone in the house in whatever way he could.

As Mr Thornton's landlord at Marlborough Mill, Mr Bell went to visit him a few times and even dined there one evening. He was an astute old fellow and in no time he was able to ascertain that Carrie had feelings for Mr Thornton, though he was unsure why they were not together, and that Margaret had feelings for the MP, Mr Southard.

As such, when Margaret's aunt, Mrs Shaw came to take her back to London, Mr Bell informed Mrs Shaw that as her Godfather, Mr Bell was taking responsibility for Margaret's care and, for the time being at least, he intended to move to Milton, which was after all his home town, and live with the young women.

Mrs Shaw bristled but given that Mr Bell was a reputable man and at the end of the day, a man, she relented, staying only one day in Milton.

Although Margaret didn't question him while they had their altercation, once Mrs Shaw had left, Margaret had to know what he was up to.

"Mr Bell?"

"I'm sorry my dear, I know I should have

discussed this with you first but I think it perhaps best if you don't make any life-changing decisions right now. I'm willing to stay with you for a few months at least, and if you do decide that you would like to live with your Aunt Shaw, then you can leave with my blessing. However, something tells me that your future lies up here rather than down in London, am I right?"

Margaret blushed.

"I don't know. Mr Southard and I have become very friendly and I do like him very much but... well, I am not sure if I should trust my judgement at the moment."

"Quite right," Mr Bell said, taking her hand. "Which is why you should stay until your grief is less raw, then decide where your future lies."

Carrie listened to their conversation from the hallway. She hadn't meant to eavesdrop but she hadn't wanted to interrupt them either. Mr Bell really was a very sensible man, she thought, and he was right about Margaret not making any firm decisions now.

However, the thought of staying in Milton brought her both immense joy and heartache and a part of her longed to run away and leave her problems behind.

Mr Hale's funeral was a very subdued affair and despite the pain she caused him, Mr Thornton was sorry not to see Carrie here. She enjoyed defying the societal norms and he had fully expected to see her here.

When the service was over, in the course of conversation he asked Mr Bell about Miss Preston's absence.

"She wanted to stay home with Margaret. Lovely

girl, that one, very caring."

"Indeed," Mr Thornton said, though his tone was sharp.

"I can't help noticing, Thornton, that, well, perhaps there is something between you and Miss Preston."

"No," he answered curtly.

"Are you quite sure?" he pressed.

"Quite," Mr Thornton snapped. "But believe me, it is not for want of trying on my part. If you'll excuse me, Mr Bell."

"Oh, yes, of course." Mr Bell let him go, easily recognising the signs of a broken heart.

Although he was unmarried, Mr Bell was no stranger to love. Unfortunately his beloved had chosen to marry the man her parents thought best for her, someone who had both money and a title. He was no longer bitter about the experience, but he had also never loved anyone else to the same degree, and so he remained a bachelor; content to spend his days studying and teaching.

Still, that didn't mean he wanted anyone else to endure what he had gone through and whilst he was here, he vowed to do whatever it took to make Miss Preston see sense. Or at the very least, present him a reasonable argument for why she and Mr Thornton should not be together.

"Carrie, my dear?" Mr Bell said as he helped Carrie to pack up some of Mr Hale's books. Margaret had put those she wanted to keep aside and the rest were being boxed up and donated to Mr Thornton's and Mr Higgins's recent school project. Mr Thornton had offered the use of one of his sheds for use as a school room and the workers between them paid for the teacher.

They couldn't afford a proper teacher, of course, so Mr Thornton had asked the reverend if his eldest daughter might like the job, since she was educated though still unmarried and this was surely charitable work. What the children learned was basic; just reading, writing and arithmetic but it was better than nothing. Perhaps with time the school might evolve into something that could truly change lives.

The teacher was outnumbered by over thirty to one and the school was still growing, so some of the mothers who were unable to work had begun helping out. Though they could do little in the way of teaching, they too were learning and some of the more able parents could now teach the basics to the new pupils enrolling at the school.

These books were well out of the school's league but Carrie and Margaret were hopeful that one day they might be of use to the students.

"Yes, Mr Bell?"

"I hope you don't think me impertinent but I wanted to speak to you about Mr Thornton."

"What about him?"

"Well, was there something between the two of you?"

Carrie looked down at the books in her hands.

"There was," she admitted in a small voice.

"And might I ask what happened?" he asked, abandoning his books and approaching her, placing his hand on her shoulder.

"Too much," she said. "First I turned him down, then he discovered something about me that displeased him and I turned him away. Now... I don't know, Mr Bell. I feel so confused. I do care for him, still, but he also scares me and... well I am afraid I rejected him again soon after Mr Hale died. The truth is I didn't mean to on that occasion, but nevertheless I have offended him once again. I fear it is hopeless."

"Don't say that," he encouraged.

"How can I not? I... I am very different from most women in this time, Mr Bell, and I'm afraid my expectations are higher than many women."

"He is not rich enough for you?" Mr Bell asked, confused by her statement.

"Oh no," she smiled. "Money is nice but not important. No, when I say I have high expectations, I mean in how my partner treats me. I want to be an equal, not a subordinate. I want to be respected for my mind as much as my looks and I want to be able to trust my partner implicitly."

While he had never heard such demands of a man before, he thought that Mr Thornton fit the bill she described more than any other man of his acquaintance.

"And you are sure that Thornton is not the man for you?"

"Even if I could excuse his previous behaviour, Mr Bell, I honestly don't think that he would give me another chance. I have well and truly blotted my copy book, just as he has with me." She looked up into his eyes. "I fear it is hopeless."

Chapter Nineteen

For once Mr Thornton found himself listening to his sister's mindless chatter, though only because it was preferable to thinking of other matters, like how to break it to his workers that he had to close the mill. He did not much like the idea but he had few options left and if he continued running the mill, he would go into serious debt. It was better to close while he could still pay his workers rather than see them starve. He hoped that his good reputation would also help him to find a position at another mill.

It was a double tragedy really, since the measures he and Higgins had put into place were making a real difference to the worker's lives. To have to give that up now was not only a shame, the other masters would see it as the reason for the mill's failure and be even more set against implementing such measures themselves.

He constantly questioned himself over his decision not to join in with Watson's speculation but he could not fault his desire to protect his workers wages, for if he had lost money they too would have suffered for his gamble.

If only those who owed him money would pay up, then he might be able to stay open for another month or two, and there was always the slim possibility of a miracle in that time. Alas, the bank refused to increase his loan and the buyers grew slower and slower at paying their bills. The gap between the two was growing forever wider and Mr Thornton couldn't blame the bank for wanting to limit its losses.

Between his personal finances, the sale of his

machinery and the outstanding monies owed to him, he would be able to clear that loan but it would leave him with little extra. Though they would not be reduced to living in the slums, the next few years would be very hard on him and his mother. He knew she could handle it for she was a strong woman and had already coped with everything life had thrown at her but still, he desperately wished that she did not have to cope.

He and his mother were not openly affectionate but the bond between them was unbreakable and more than anything he wanted to repay her for her faith in him over the years. Without her drive and her belief in him, he would likely still be working as a shop boy.

Wanting to put off the inevitable for as long as possible he continued to listen to Fanny chatter about the latest gossip and how she was redecorating her rooms in Watson's home. With the wedding less than a month ago, she seemed to be settling into married life with surprising ease.

Though she had been less than sympathetic towards John about his refusal to participate in her husband, Watson's speculation, he couldn't find it in his heart to be angry with her. She was family and even when you had no possessions in the world, you still had a family. Though she was superficial and flighty, he knew that she loved him and their mother.

When she finally took her leave of them, John kissed her cheek and smiled at her.

"I am glad that you are happy with Watson," he said, meaning every word, for to see her suffer from the loss of the mill would be more than he could bear. Fanny did not have the strength of him or their mother and this time she would be old enough to feel the shame of their misfortune. He was sure that such hardship would crush her.

Fanny looked surprised at his kiss and smiled uneasily, for her brother was not given to displays of affection.

Once she had left, he returned to his office, his shoulders more sloped than usual as he crossed the yard, as though he was carrying the weight of the world on them. He considered calling Higgins into his office now to tell him but he wasn't quite ready to face the disappointment he would see in the other man's eyes. Higgins needed this job more than most, for unlike most of the workers, the other mills wouldn't hire him because of his association with the union.

Instead, Mr Thornton picked up his post and began opening it.

He missed working with Carrie, for she handled his office with such efficiency that he now felt slightly lost without her. Everything still got done of course, and he still used the systems she had put in place but it took longer without her help and if he was honest, just watching her work had a calming influence on him. She was like a soothing balm and nothing was ever quite so bad as it should be while she was around.

He missed her, now more than ever. Of course even if they were still on speaking terms, she would likely want nothing to do with him now that the mill had failed. Now that he had failed. He gave a weary sigh and reached for the next envelope, surprised to note that it was in her handwriting. He forgot about the rest of his mail for the moment and sat back to read her letter.

Dear Mr Thornton,

I know about the difficulties your mill is facing as

a result of the fallout from the strike and how difficult the markets are at the moment. I also know that soon you will have little option but to close the mill and sack your workers.

Mr Watson recently offered you a speculation which I am sure you considered as a possibility to solve your financial problems. As you will no doubt be aware by now, the venture was successful.

I knew that you would not invest though, not only because of your family history but also because you are far too principled to risk harming others with such an uncertain venture.

I also know of the good you have been doing for the workers, since Mr Higgins was often telling Mr Hale of the wondrous schemes that you and he are implementing. It is to your credit that you are actively seeking to better the lives of your workers and as such it is a very bitter pill to swallow that just when you are finally achieving some real good, you will be forced to close your doors.

As such, I took the liberty of investing on your behalf.

Please rest assured that I have the initial stake I invested back in full and that I have also made a healthy profit from my own investment.

Enclosed is a bankers draft for your share of the profit. I hope this will be enough to keep your mill running and I wish you every luck in the future.

Yours sincerely,

Carrie Preston

He looked at the enclosed bankers draft and was so shocked by the amount that he had to look a second time to be sure. This was no small gesture, this was a substantial amount of money, one that would solve all of his financial difficulties.

What did this mean though? Was she reaching out

to him, trying to make amends? Or was she doing this to salve her conscience?

If he had to guess, he would say the latter but if he was right and she was feeling guilty, perhaps that meant that she knew that she had been making excuses not to be with him.

He also remembered Higgins telling him that Carrie had advised him to speak to Mr Thornton, saying that he was an honourable man.

He almost dare not think it, for if he was wrong he would be devastated but perhaps it meant that she was willing to forgive him; perhaps it meant he still had a chance.

Mr Bell had approached him once on her behalf but, still stinging from her most recent rebuttal, he had refused to speak of the matter, cutting Mr Bell short and being rather rude to his friend. Now though he began to think that perhaps he had been premature. Perhaps Mr bell knew something that he did not.

And even if he didn't know anything, he had been living in the same house as Carrie and might be able to shed some light on her behaviour.

Before he could think about it too much, he set about arranging to see his landlord.

Carrie was playing her piano when she heard the doorbell ring. She didn't think anything of it since she had a pupil due shortly and she continued to play while Dixon answered the door. The song was one of her favourites, though it was a very melancholy tune. She lacked the voice to do the song justice so she just played an instrumental version, enjoying the melody and silently singing the lyrics in her head. She'd been playing this song a lot recently, so much so that the other evening Mr

Bell had asked her if she was all right since the tune was so sad. She had assured him that she was fine but on more than one occasion recently she had been reduced to tears while playing.

The song had a special resonance for her now. It reminded her of how she used to scorn her family and blame them for so much; now she longed to be able to argue with them again. She wondered what her Aunt Immy would think of the mess she had made of things here. Immy had given her the chance of a lifetime and here she was, miserable by her own hand. She had begun to think that perhaps she had overreacted when she sent Mr Thornton away, perhaps his reaction had been understandable and she was simply being a coward, as usual.

When she finished the song she heard someone clapping behind her and turned to see Mr Thornton standing in the doorway. Her heart skipped a beat and her stomach filled with butterflies as she looked at him, for she really did love him more than she could say.

Chapter Twenty

"That was beautiful," Mr Thornton said. "Sad but very lovely."

Carrie swallowed her feelings down and tried to remember why she didn't like him.

"If you are here to give me the money back, I won't accept it. You need to swallow your pride and take it for the good of your workers as well as yourself."

"Well that told me," he said, his voice warm. "I thank you for your faith in me, Miss Preston" He had decided to keep the money since he did view it as a sign of her faith in him and he would not throw that gesture back in her face. He also thought that she expected him to fight her over the money, but Mr Thornton had learned his lesson and had no desire to ever fight with her again.

"It's nothing. Now if you'll excuse me, I have a pupil arriving shortly."

"No you don't. Forgive me but Mr Bell told me that you teach Sarah Caulfield today, so I paid a visit to her mother and asked her to cancel her daughter's lesson this week. I explained that I needed to see you on an urgent matter of business."

"I believe we have discussed our business."

"Perhaps, but I have been trying to understand why you are so afraid of me."

"I... I have told you why." She looked down at her hands where they rested in her lap.

"Yes, but I don't believe you," he said, stepping further into the room and closing the door behind him. "I don't think that you are afraid that I will harm you."

"No?"

"No. I also don't think you stayed with Mark for so long because you didn't want to be alone. I think you stayed with him because you didn't love him."

Angered by his words, Carrie looked up at him.

"Don't be stupid."

"I don't think it is stupid, Carrie." He was slowly edging closer to her, almost as if she was a wild animal that he needed to be cautious around. "You told me your society is more evolved that mine and that it studied relationships, but if that's true I don't think that you gained much insight from it. I think that you felt safe with Mark because you didn't love him. He can't break your heart if you don't love him."

Carrie looked uncomfortable but she didn't deny it.

"I think that I terrify you because of how much you love me; because you know that I could break your heart."

"You already have," she said sadly.

"As you have broken mine, on more than one occasion. And I have already apologised for ny previous behaviour. I think you know me by now, Carrie, and I think that you know my behaviour then was out of character."

"You hurt me once, you could do it again."

"Yes, but then it's not every day that you find out your beloved is from somewhere so very different. There is a reason you haven't told anyone else where you are truly from, Carrie, and that's because you fear their reaction. You understand that everyone else would be shocked and yet you allow me no leeway at all to come to terms with your revelation."

"Do you think it's easy for me to put up with living in this backwards time where I'm considered little more than chattel?"

"No, I do not," he said, keeping his voice warm and reasonable. "I have seen you getting angry at the restrictions placed on you, resenting the judgements others make about your behaviour."

Carrie looked at him, wondering where he was going with this.

"You told me that you had read about my time and my life in history books, so I could argue that you knew what to expect when you came here and have no right to be angry."

"Reading something and living it are two very different things," she said.

"Quite," he agreed. "And yet, although I have not had the luxury of reading about your time, I am expected to accept it with perfect equanimity. To not bat an eyelid at the lack of clothing or loose morals, to simply understand that things are different in your time, even though I have never experienced your life in any way."

She realised that he was right, she had been expecting an awful lot of him. In fact, considering how angry many things in this time made her, she was a hypocrite herself for not allowing Mr Thornton a little anger when he discovered how different the place she came from was.

"When did you become so insightful?" she asked.

"Around the time that you broke my heart, and your own."

She was about to reply but he cut her off.

"Don't deny it, your misery is etched into every feature. Perhaps those who don't know you well can be fooled but not me. I know the pain you feel because I feel it too, every hour of every day."

He had been getting closer and closer to her and now he stopped a few feet away.

"I know that trusting me is a risk, Carrie, and I know that I have behaved shamefully but look at me; I am a broken man. I will never love another, as I am sure you will not either. Why should we continue to be miserable when what we want is ours for the taking?"

"You make it sound easy," she said.

"It isn't. I know it's frightening for you. Once we are wed you will cease to have any rights as an individual and in the eyes of the law, you will be nothing more than my wife. Your property will be considered mine and my word will always trump yours."

She nodded, for he was right and that was how marriage worked here.

"Do you honestly think the letter of the law means anything to me?" he asked her. "Just because it says I can overrule you, does not mean that I ever would. The look of hurt I would see on your face is a bigger deterrent than any punishment you could dream up. I am also shrewd enough to realise that you are strong and independent. I have no doubt that if I were to ever mistreat you that, lawful or not, you would leave me and probably do a more than fair job of keeping yourself hidden from me."

"I would," she confirmed.

"And I wouldn't have it any other way," he assured her. "For any man who would mistreat you does not deserve you, myself included. I will never risk losing you."

Carrie could feel herself giving in to his words, wanting to believe him and wishing that she had the courage to fall into his arms.

"I love you, Carrie Preston and I always will, whether you accept me or not. I suspect that you will always love me also, so let us end each other's torment and take a chance."

Carrie felt tears stinging her eyes. She so much wanted to believe what he said.

"I don't know if I can," she said honestly.

"I am not asking for much," he said, taking another step closer. "Not yet at least. Let me court you, Carrie, treat you as a lady should be treated and prove to you that I will never hurt you."

"I don't know."

"Yes you do but you're scared. Don't let that fear keep you from the life we could have, Carrie. Fight back, fight for me, fight for us. I know you are capable of it."

His eyes were so warm and filled with such love and tenderness that she found herself wanting to trust him, only the words wouldn't come. Instead she suddenly reached out and grasped him, wrapping her arms around his waist and laying her head against his chest. John wrapped his arms around her also.

"Be careful, Carrie, for if you do not speak I shall claim you as my own. If I must go, send me away now and do not continue my torment."

"Stay," she managed to say.

John's heart soared and for the first time in a long while his smile was genuine. Slowly he pulled away slightly and, placing one finger under her chin, gently tilted her head up. She didn't resist and slowly he bent his head and kissed her softly. To his immense relief, she responded. When he pulled away she was also smiling.

"I'm sorry," she said.

"As am I," he agreed. "But let us not waste time dwelling on our wrongs, they are in the past. Come for a walk with me and tell me more of where you are from."

"Are you sure you want to hear it?"

"That place created you. Beautiful, wonderful, obstinate, strong and courageous you. I want to know everything about such a place, no matter how alien."

He slipped his hand into hers and silently they headed out for a walk. Strangely they did not speak for a long while, only sneaking glances at each other and smiling when each caught the other staring. They headed to the hill and stopped when near the top to look down over Milton. Carrie wrapped one arm around his waist and leaned into him as he wrapped his arm around her shoulders.

She looked down on the town below her and silently thanked her Aunt Immy for this gift.

"Do you think I'm crazy?" she asked him.

"Absolutely certifiable," he said, though his voice was warm with mirth.

"What does that make you then?" she asked.

"A raving lunatic?" he suggested.

"Then at least we're in good company." She tightened her hold on him.

Yes, she thought to herself, she was exactly where she was supposed to be.

"Though if you really want to talk about crazy, you should have met my Aunt Imelda."

By unspoken agreement they sat down on the hillside and John listened with a mixture of amusement and awe as Carrie told him all about her favourite aunt; how she was the black sheep of the family, how oddly she dressed, how wildly she behaved and finally, how she had granted Carrie her heart's desire, namely the chance to be with Mr John Thornton.

When she was done she looked up at the sky.

"So what do you think, Aunt Imm?" she asked

aloud. "Did I do good?"

Only slightly perturbed by Carrie talking to a dead woman he drew her close to him and kissed her cheek.

Carrie heart skipped a beat as she thought she heard her aunt's hearty laugh, though it was soft, as though carried on a breeze. Maybe it was real or maybe she had imagined it, but either way she took it as a good sign.

Epilogue: Ten Years Later

Carrie was on tenterhooks as she waited, pacing the floor of their home. Those around her were already in the party mood and drinking quite happily, regardless of the outcome. They showed none of her worry. She couldn't drink yet though, for she was so nervous that she wasn't sure she could keep it down.

Finally Margaret approached her and Carrie smiled, for Margaret was an old hand at these.

"Relax," Margaret smiled sweetly. "I am sure he was successful."

"That's easy for you to say, you've done this before. How do you stand it?" Carrie asked. "What if he doesn't get in? He will be crushed."

"He will survive," Margaret assured her friend. "If there is one thing that I have learned about Milton men, and women for that matter, it is that they are survivors. John will simply pick himself up, dust himself off and continue on as normal. In another five years he will try again, having learned from any mistakes made this time."

"You are right, of course," Carrie gave a deep sigh.

"But this is beside the point, John is a, what it is you say, a shoo-in?"

"Yes." Carrie smiled, she loved hearing her modern slang on Margaret's lips. "So, how is Bernard doing?"

"He is well, I am sure. And this is his fourth election so he is an old hand at it now."

"I wish they would let us go with them."

"I am sure that they want time to compose themselves should they lose, not to mention time to celebrate with cigars and brandy if they should win."

"I wouldn't mind cigars and brandy," Carrie said with a wry smile.

"Carrie, you have always worked, even when you were with with child, you have virtually taken over this mill during the campaign and I don't see you giving way to a manager once John is elected. You must allow them to keep some traditional male practices to themselves."

Carrie smiled, conceding the point.

"You know, I could give in much more gracefully were I certain of the result," she teased.

"Mama?"

Carrie turned to see her daughter coming into the room. She looked beautiful, dressed up as the adults were, ready to celebrate with her parents should fortune favour her father.

Carrie could see a few of the guests casting their wary eyes at her children all evening, for having children at an adult gathering was very unseemly.

"Laura, darling," she bent to kiss her daughter's cheek and wrapped her arms around the girl, taking comfort in the quick hug. "Where is your brother?"

"He's in the kitchen," she answered. "Cook is making us some warm milk."

"Are you getting tired?" Carrie asked, for though the children had pleaded to be allowed to wait up for their father and had risen late this morning, they were only seven and nine and the time was nearing midnight.

Laura nodded.

"Well why don't you have your milk," Carrie suggested, "get changed-"

"But I want to see daddy!" she protested.

"If you let me finish!" Carrie chided gently. "Get

changed then go and sleep in our bed. That way we'll have to wake you and let you know the result when we come to bed."

Laura thought about that for a moment then nodded. Facially she was the spitting image of her mother, only with her fathers colouring; dark, almost black hair and piercing blue eyes. She would break many a heart as she grew older. Her younger brother, Daniel, could almost be John's twin rather than his son, and had very little of his mother in his features. He did however have a lot of her in his personality. He was a shy and somewhat timid boy, but he had a huge heart and showed much courage when overcoming his fears.

It helped that his elder sister was always around and very protective of her little brother. Carrie thought that he would be destined for a scholarly life rather than one working in the mills, though she knew that was hypocritical of her.

Carrie was not destined for a life working in a mill; she found the noise, the workers and the activity intimidating but her desire to be independent, to work and contribute to their family and their business had helped her to overcome those fears. It was quite possible that Daniel would also find that strength.

Laura on the other hand was a born leader. With all her father's charisma and forceful personality, it wouldn't surprise Carrie if Laura should end up the first female MP, especially given how interested she had been in her father's campaign. Still, both children were young and Carrie had no intention of forcing any profession on them. They would always have her support no matter what path they chose in life.

Laura went off to the kitchen and Carrie was just

about to speak to Margaret again when she heard hooves on the cobblestones in the courtyard. Her heart skipped a beat and unconsciously both women reached for the others hand, equally fearful of hearing bad news.

Carrie swallowed down her fears as best she could and squeezed Margaret's hand, both giving and receiving strength from the gesture.

John and Bernard entered the room together, both looking glum. Carrie's heart sank for John would be devastated if he had lost. She felt Margaret grip her hand harder, almost to the point of pain but she didn't complain.

John raised his voice and called for quiet, for having already imbibed much alcohol, many of the partygoers had not even noticed their entrance. A hush quickly fell over the room since most were sensible enough to understand what his dour expression must mean.

"Ladies and Gentlemen, I hope you have had a good evening so far," John began. "But I fear we are about to eclipse that." Suddenly he broke out in a broad smile. "I give you the Right Honourable Bernard Southard, the returning member of parliament for Lampton," he raised Bernard's hand and the guests clapped and cheered.

"And I," Bernard interrupted the cheers. "Would like to present to you the Right Honourable John Thornton, the new member of parliament for Milton!"

Carrie actually screamed a little as she launched herself at her husband, wrapping her arms around his neck and holding him tightly.

"You evil man!" she chided though she was laughing. "You had me worried there."

"You doubted me?" he teased.

Carrie pulled back and cupped his face.

"You? Never. Those charged with voting for you? I wouldn't trust them as far as I could throw them."

John laughed and hugged her again.

"You realise that this means you will have to take on more responsibility at the mill," he said.

"I think I'm up to the challenge," she answered.

"Are you certain?"

"Of course, I have had a very good teacher."

She pulled away and smiled at him but pretty soon he was swept sway from her by the other partygoers who wished to congratulate him. Carrie used the opportunity to go in search of her children, who she found sitting at the kitchen table with Cook.

Both children looked up eagerly as she entered and her smile told them all they needed to know.

"Cook wouldn't let us go until we finished our milk," Laura pouted.

"She is right, you shouldn't be wasteful. Now drink up and we can go and see Daddy for a short while; then it is time for bed."

"But I'm not tired," both children wailed in unison.

"Then you can stay up until I see a yawn, at which point you will both be whisked off to bed, agreed?"

"Yes, Mama."

"I'm so pleased," Cook said. "I was hopeful when we heard the ruckus upstairs but it's nice to know for certain."

Carrie smiled at her and gave a relieved sigh.

"I think I would have gone mad if I'd had to wait much longer."

"Would you like a tipple, ma'am, to calm your nerves?"

"Oh, I don't think I can face alcohol right now, but I'd love a mug of warm milk if there's any left. My stomach has been turning somersaults for hours and that might help settle it."

"Or at least help you make butter if it doesn't," Cook joked as she poured another mug of milk from the pan still on the stove. Her mistress had some unusual ideas but she was very affable and Cook was inclined to like her.

When the children were finished, Cook escorted them upstairs so that Carrie could enjoy a few minutes of silence by the fire to calm her frayed nerves as she sipped her milk.

It had been a long few weeks of campaigning and worry and though she was pleased by John's victory, the fatigue had finally caught up with her, as she had no doubt it would also catch up with John in the next few hours.

"Hiding already?"

She heard his dulcet tone and turned towards the doorway where he was standing.

"That's your party up there," she reminded him.

"And I can leave it if I want to," he countered. "Especially when the only person I want to celebrate with is right here."

"Where are the children?" she asked.

"The last I saw them, they were practising giving speeches to anyone who would listen."

"Even Daniel?"

"It was Daniel's idea."

"I'd be careful if I were you," she teased. "In a few years he might give you some competition."

John took the other seat by the fire and reached out to take her hand. Though he was clearly feeling tired, his smile was still bright and never completely left his face.

"Can you believe it?" he asked. "Me, an M.P.?"

"I can believe it. You are a magistrate after all, and even though you have a wild and uncouth wife, you are still well-respected by the local business men."

"Wild and uncouth?" he questioned knowing that it was not a phrase she would usually use and that she had obviously overheard it being spoken in reference to her. Her futuristic ways did often invite scorn from many of her peers but they also invited respect from a few forward-thinking men and women.

As though to show him just how wild and uncouth she could be, she left her seat and settled herself on his lap. John was used to her forward behaviour now and even quite enjoyed it. She was usually very careful to keep such displays relatively private, though she wasn't above giving him a quick kiss in public. Most women privately ridiculed her for such forward behaviour but most men of his acquaintance envied him a wife who expressed her affection so freely.

John's arms found their way around her waist to hold her to him and she kissed him deeply, a display of affection what would make any servant who happened upon them blush a deep shade of crimson! John found he wasn't in the mood to care though. To his surprise, she then offered him some of her drink, holding the mug to his lips for him as though he were a child. Again, this behaviour was very inappropriate but over the years, instead of educating her on the proper decorum of this time, he had instead been educated in the ways of Carrie's world and had discovered that in many arenas, he much preferred her way of doing things.

"Milk?" he said, having drunk a sip without

knowing what was in the mug. "This is supposed to be a party, woman!"

Carrie smiled.

"My stomach wasn't up to anything stronger," she confessed.

She finished her drink and then kissed him again.

"Better?" he asked.

"I think I might be able to raise a glass of champagne in your honour now," she smiled. "How long do you think until we can kick everyone out and have our own celebration?"

"I fear we will have to accommodate them for a while longer, given that many of them have supported me during the campaign."

"Very well." Carrie pouted. "But I feel it only right to warn you that you will not be setting a foot out of this house tomorrow. I want you all to myself for a day."

John smiled. Very little would be expected of him tomorrow since almost everyone here tonight would be nursing a sore head. John wasn't much given to excessive drinking since it upset his ability to made decisions. Tomorrow he would have no hangover (as Carrie called the after effects of excessive drinking) but for once he found himself grateful for the excesses of others since it meant few, if any demands would be made of him.

"I think I can oblige you there," he smiled wickedly at her.

Carrie laughed and got off his lap. She held her hand out to him and he allowed her to pull him to his feet.

"I'm proud of you," she said, wrapping her arms around his waist, not quite ready to return to the party yet. "And your mother would have been proud too, you know."

"Thank you," he said, kissing the top of her head and holding her tightly.

There were many important people upstairs, more powerful, wealthier and more respected than his wife but now that his mother was gone, it was only Carrie's good opinion that he cared about keeping. He sought her advice on almost everything and if he hadn't had her full support, he would not have even considered running for parliament.

Hannah Thornton had lived to see both of their children born, as well as three of Fanny's five children, before she finally succumbed to a nasty bout of pneumonia. If she could be here now though, Carrie was in little doubt that she would be the proudest woman in all of England at this moment. John missed her dearly and though their relationship had never been exactly easy, even Carrie missed her, for anyone so wholly on John's side couldn't be all bad.

"I could always throw a fainting spell," Carrie said, her voice slightly muffled by his jacket. "Then you would be obliged to care for me and leave the party."

"Oh, do not tempt me, you wicked woman," he smiled and removed his arms from about her. "Come on, let's get it over with."

He took her hand and they headed back to the party. She stayed at his side for most of the evening and was every inch the elegant hostess, making conversation with even the most boorish people there. She excused herself for a few minutes to tuck the children into bed then returned to his side and made what would otherwise have been a tedious evening bearable, even pleasant for him.

Finally at around 2 o'clock the party began to break up. Carrie and John congratulated Margaret and Bernard once again and thanked them for all their help with the campaign, then finally they closed the door behind the last guest and headed upstairs to their bedroom.

Carrie undressed, took her hair down and climbed under the covers to wait for John to join her. He slid under the covers a few moments later and Carrie curled into him, resting her head on his chest.

"I do hope you're not expecting anything from me tonight," he said, only half joking.

Carrie raised her head and looked up at him.

"Why do you think you're under house arrest tomorrow?" she asked, a mischievous twinkle in her eye.

"Have I told you lately that I love you?" he asked, smiling at her words.

"I believe you have, but frequent reminders are always welcome," she teased. "I love you too, you know?"

"I do," he assured her. He put his hand on her head and gently pressed down, encouraging her to lie back against him. "Now sleep," he urged her. "You can have your wicked way with me until your heart's content tomorrow."

"Mm," she agreed as she snuggled against him. "I'll hold you to that," she assured him, a playful smile still on her lips when she drifted off to sleep a few moments later.

About the Author

Cat Winchester was born in East Anglia. After trying many
different places, she is now happily settled in Edinburgh,
with her family and three dogs.

www.cswinchester.net

CPSIA information can be obtained at www.ICGtesting.com
Printed in the USA
BVOW011907090512

289818BV00009B/3/P